A Different Kind of Freedom: A Romani Story

RICHARD O'NEILL

Series Consultant:
Tony Bradman

SCHOLASTIC

AUTHOR'S NOTE

'Three—nil down!'

One of the reasons I wanted to write this book is because I love the game of football. The other reason is because former England player Rab Howell is a real-life hero of mine and also the hero of Lijah, this book's lead character.

Although a hundred years apart, Rab and I, we have a number of things in common. We both worked in professional league football – he was a player and I was a trainer. And we were both born and brought up in traditional nomadic Romani communities in the north of England.

Writing this book allowed me to look at the history of professional football from a unique angle. It reminded me that, if you come from a marginalized community, you often have a number of challenges to overcome. Or to use a football analogy: you're starting the game a couple of goals down.

Sometimes these challenges also come from within your own community, if you're trying to achieve something unusual for the community – perhaps from your parents or other family members who disapprove on cultural grounds or simply don't understand why you have chosen such a path. These can be the biggest obstacles to overcome as you are now *starting the game three rather than two–nil down*.

Just like Lijah, I too had to deal with challenges when it came to being involved in football, but also like him I found my desire for the sport was too much to deny. As tough as things can sometimes seem, remember that, just as in every football game, no matter how many goals down you are – until the final whistle blows, you are always in with a chance of winning.

I hope Lijah's journey provides inspiration for your own journey.

Richard O'Neill

PS If you come across a word or phrase that you've never heard of before, flick to the back of the book for a dictionary of Romani terms.

One

"C'mon, get that horse yoked up, you two! We're wasting the best part of the day."

Henry and I were hunkered down around the fire in the middle of the camp, trying to get the last bits of warmth from it. It would be freezing on the flat cart, but it wouldn't do us any good to keep our dad waiting.

January and February were always the hardest months for us. The weather was cold, often freezing for days on end. "Hard on the animals and us," as my Uncle Billy would say. But as hard as life was living in wooden wagons with canvas tops and in tents made of old ships' sails, it was all we knew and we liked it: the freedom and the love of our family. We prided ourselves on being healthy and strong and looking out for ourselves. "I have healthy babies, I do," my mam would tell anyone who would listen. She was known to give her advice to other Traveller and non-Traveller – or *Gorja* – women alike on how to raise strong children.

Reluctantly, Henry and I rose from beside the fire. We pulled the belts tight on our woollen coats and our caps down tight on our heads, fastened the heavy leather harness on to the horse, backed him into the cart and led him out across the frozen ground, on to the cobbled street, where the metal-rimmed wheels and the horse's shoes competed to make the loudest clattering.

"No one sleeps while we're around, eh?" said my dad, always one to try to make a joke. It made me smile, but the joke really was that no one would be asleep at this time anyway. People would either already be at work in the steel mill or one of the other factories, or else getting their children ready for school.

All three of us walked alongside, until the horse picked up a bit of speed and we could jump onto the cart.

We were going out to collect old clothes and metal, or anything else that could be swapped or sold: a chair with a broken leg, a metal lamp that wasn't working properly. 'Rag-and-bone', the settled people called it. We knew it as *tattin*.

I liked this part of the day. It was full of possibilities; we could come back with a full cart or with hardly anything.

"That's the life of the Traveller people," my dad

2

would always remind us.

Closer to the city, the roads grew busier with the horses and carts of delivery people and tradesmen going about their business. We stopped to let a tram go past. Three boys were hanging off the back of it. They spotted us and began holding their noses.

"Dirty Gypsies!" one of them shouted. The others broke out into exaggerated laughter. My dad and Henry pretended not to hear them, but I couldn't help scowling, giving them the 'evil eye', as some people called it.

This kind of name-calling was something that happened to us regularly and something we tried to ignore, but it still hurt. Although we did dirty work, we weren't dirty people. We were in fact the opposite, as my mam had us washing properly and wearing clean clothes, whether it was winter or summer.

The first time I'd heard name-calling, I was only little. When I asked my dad why people did it, he said, "'Cause they don't know any better. We ain't Gypsies; we're Romani people – Travellers – an' we've been here longer than most of them."

"The settled people give us things though, don't they?" I said, confused.

"Aye, they do," replied my dad darkly, "but only things they don't want any more."

That had been back when we lived in North Yorkshire, where I was born. I preferred the quiet of the countryside there, but my dad and mam had wanted to move to Sheffield. Mam for her side of the family and Dad because there was more money to be earned here. He was right about that at least. I was four years old when we'd set up camp with our wagons and tents on the outskirts of the city, in a place called Ecclesfield. On looking down at Sheffield for the first time, I pointed towards the city, where the street lights were making the dark sky glow yellow and the factories were sending out their smoke, making loud hissing and grinding noises.

"What's that?" I asked my dad.

"That's the *baro wafti gav* and it's coming to get us, eatin' us up bit by bit," my dad said laughing.

"Don't scare the *chavvies* with that kind of *radgeness*," my mam scolded. "The big bad city isn't coming to get any of us. It's called progress and we won't be earning the living we need without it."

"I'm only joking," he answered. But I knew he wasn't. I was to learn later that he was the one scared of the factories: of dealing with the changes that we were already experiencing and would continue to experience as the age of machines and factories raced on around us. I know he felt the difference

4

between us and the settled people more than any of us. We were, after all, very different. We spoke a different language, we looked different, and we lived differently to them. From a very young age I was interested in where we had come from. My old grandma, our *phuri dai*, would laugh and say, "Only the good Lord knows that an' he's too high and mighty to tell the likes of us." Then she'd go on to tell us about when she was a young girl and about our great grandparents and back even further than that. She couldn't read or write but she knew every year, every month and every day when something important happened; she knew all the kings and queens all the way from King Henry VIII. "Our people danced for him," she'd often tell us and I would try hard to imagine people like us at a castle.

The day was cold, but the sun shone and even had a little warmth in it. We went about our work happily. My dad stood on the cart, rang a bell, then shouted, "Rag-and-bone!"

His cries brought people to the doors of their houses and Henry and I went to pick up the things they gave us. We'd gone to the streets on the other side of the city to our camp, where there were bigger houses – it was pointless going to some streets as people were so poor. A few times, when we'd gone on to a street where people clearly had nothing to give, my dad had taken pity on them and handed out a few of the clothes we'd collected. We all knew that my dad was a hard man with a soft heart. Today was going well, however. By the time we stopped to have a bit of dinner – some bread and cheese my mam had put in a brown paper bag for us all to share – my brother Henry had already been given some old broken brass lamps and I'd managed to get an armful of good quality men's suits, which looked hardly worn. We'd sell these down at the clothes shop. The cart was so full that Henry and I had to walk alongside it, while my dad sat on the edge at the front, driving the horse as we walked, tired but happy, back towards the camp. Our good spirits did not last long.

Two

We already knew there was something wrong when we got within earshot of the camp. It was too quiet. My dad handed the reins to Henry and walked towards the fire, where my mam was stirring whatever was cooking in a big black pot. As we parked the cart up, we heard my dad's raised voice.

"Too many people come round poking their *nak* into our business, Kushy," he said using my mam's name which meant it was serious. Everyone knew my mam as Kushy, a nickname she got when she was little and trying to say the word *kushti*, which means very good. My brother Henry was named after my dad, because he was christened Henry, even though everyone knew him as Abe, probably because there was too many Henrys in the family already. I was called Lijah after the man in the Bible.

Henry glanced over at me. "Those census people – the people from the local authority – they must have been round again," he muttered.

I swallowed. The census people collected information on everybody who lived in houses and they made sure they did it to Travellers too. The last time they had come round with the police, they'd told my mam and dad I needed to be in school, otherwise they'd alert the school board.

"There ain't no point in him going to school," my dad snapped, proving Henry right. "He never learned nowt anyway – he ain't going to be a scholar, is he?"

My mam hissed. "D'ya want the school board man around again, Abe? Next time, he said he'll have you in front of the magistrate and, mark my words, he'll do it."

"Why can't these people leave us alone? Our Lijah is nearly too old for school. He ain't going to get a job like the other boys, anyway, he's going to work with me. Did you tell them that?"

"Of course I did, but it doesn't make any difference to them. It's their rules and they will call the law on us."

"I don't want him picking up *Gorja* ways – talking like them or acting like them with all their *radgeness – dinlos*."

"Well, I'm sick and tired of havin' to up sticks and shift to another town when the school board people are out," said my mam, angrily stirring the pot.

"I've had years of it, an' I'm not doing it no more. The animals in the fields have a better life than us."

"If they won't leave us alone, there's gonna be trouble one day, Kushy," my dad said, using her name and raising his voice louder still.

My mam was straight back at him, raising hers to match. "You need to be careful talking like that. You'll get us lifted by the *moskerers*," she warned him.

Henry and I stayed standing behind the wagon, listening. We both knew my mam must be really worried, for her to mention the police. They were no friends of ours.

My mam called us over to the fire, signalling the end of the argument between her and my dad. My mam and dad rarely argued, but whenever they did it seemed to come to an end as quickly as it started. We took a seat on the wooden stool and waited for our mam to hand out bowls of the stew she'd been cooking.

As I ate, I thought back to my first day at school. I'd just turned seven; Henry was ten going on eleven. Anywhere else, he'd only have had a short time to go before his schooling finished, or he might even have already left, but where we lived in Sheffield we had to go until we were thirteen. It was a damp late

October morning when we'd left the camp and neither Henry nor I were looking forward to the day ahead. To keep our spirits up, we talked about the fun we'd had during the previous summer, swimming in the clearest, freshest water up in the Derbyshire hills and running about in the sunshine with our shirts off. We'd been outside from dawn until dusk and still had the tan on our faces from it.

That summer was just a happy memory now, but just the mention of school made me shudder and gave me a sick feeling in my stomach. School for me was like putting a wild animal in a circus and making it perform, the trainer being cruel to it when it couldn't do what it was told. I vowed never to visit a circus in my life.

The other people around the fire eating stew were Henry, one of my aunts, two of my uncles, a few of my little cousins, one of my older ones Urania, and my *phuri dai*. Behind us, arranged in a circle, were two large wooden wagons we called *vardos*, and four sail-cloth tents pitched between them. The adults who owned wagons slept in them along with their babies and young children, or *bitti chavvies*, as we called them. Our uncles and aunts who didn't own wagons slept in the tents. The bigger ones like us slept in tents too – Urania slept in her own tent as did me and Henry. Even if we'd have been brothers and sister, our Romani rules meant we couldn't have shared a tent with Urania.

We had parked the wagons and pitched the tents in such a way that the woodland behind us protected us from the worst of the wind blowing off the surrounding hills. I loved the forest with its mixture of trees. Whenever the world got too loud or busy for me, I went to the woods and it soothed me. I used to imagine that the big trees with their dark trunks were guards who protected us. The trees also provided us with fuel for the fire and, on the edges, there were willows growing, which we used to make many of the wooden items we sold.

When we finished our stew and handed the bowls back to my mam, my dad stood up and stretched.

"Time for you little 'uns to *jall ter woodrus*," he said, as he always did at this time of evening. Once the little children had gone to bed, there would be time for us older ones to sit some more, drink some hot, sweet *meskie* and listen to my father's instructions on what we were going to do the following day. This could be anything from delivering a horse, picking one up, selling the wooden things we made door to door or going out *tattin*, as we had done earlier that day. In the summer, once we'd got our instructions, we could stay up as late as we wanted, sharing jokes, listening to the men talk and learning how to be men ourselves. The women and children had gone to bed tired after doing their last chores of the day; we still had our last checks of the animals to do before we could turn in. In the winter, most people just wanted to get into a warm bed as soon as possible.

Due to the earlier argument, we still hadn't finished unloading the cart and sorting out the things we'd collected. It was too late to do it now; we'd have to do it at first light. I went to bed wishing that the spring would come soon.

Three

Our stories were best told around the fire. That night was no exception.

My dad would go first. He didn't have to ask us if we were listening because as soon as he got his pipe out, lit it, sucked in a puff of smoke and blew it back out, we knew that was the sign that he was going to tell us some stories. And the most important one was where we came from.

"Nearly a thousand years ago our people lived in a far-off land and we spoke the same language we do now," this would be the cue for him to test us on our Romani language, which we called Romanes, to make sure we weren't replacing it all with English. For the benefit of the little children, he'd start a game where he pointed to his head and then his eyes and worked his way all the way down to his boots, but everyone joined in laughing and sometimes saying the words in a funny way which made my dad laugh too. Once satisfied we'd completed the game properly, he would carry on with his story. "There was an emperor who took over the land where the Romani people lived. This land was a beautiful land of high mountains with snow on the tops of them even in the summer; the water was ice cold and the freshest you've ever tasted. In the summer it was hot and when the rain came down it did so hard and fast. Our people were the storytellers, the woodworkers, the metal workers, but this new emperor wanted everyone settled so he could keep an eye on them, make them work only for him. Some of them couldn't live like that, so they set off travelling across the world and some of them came into England when King Henry VIII was the king and he was bad for Gypsy people. He was the one who got where we came from wrong and said we were Egyptians and that's how we got the name Gypsies instead of Romani people."

When my dad finished this part, he would stand up, hold out his hand and — looking at my mam — say "Queen Kushy, may I have this dance," and he and she would pretend they were king and queen. We'd all clap and laugh until we could laugh no more.

We always kept a lot of animals around the camp: hens, goats, dogs and horses; our main source of transport. Depending on whether the horses had been raised by us from foals or bought to sell on, they were either tethered with a loose leather collar around their neck, attached to a chain that was fixed into the ground with a metal pole, or they were hobbled with sackcloth tied gently around their front legs so they could only move slowly. Our horses rarely tried to wander off, but they could get spooked by thunder and lightning. A horse could easily damage itself – break a leg, even – and then that'd be the end of it.

My dad was proud of the horses and ponies he bred and trained, but his dream was to breed a champion trotting horse. He'd been trying to get the money together to buy a decent foal or yearling and he was convinced that he would find the right one at a fair.

"I'll know it when I see it," he'd say and my mam would smile, having heard him say this many times before.

We had a number of bantam hens which were adept at finding food for themselves for most of the year, but in the winter we'd boil up potato peelings and a bit of grain to make a mash for them. This meant they provided us with enough eggs for our needs all year round. They were smaller and more colourful than the usual farmyard hens, raised to be able to travel well and live outside. The cockerel, who all the hens followed, made sure that they flew up on to the branch of a tree to roost at night, out of harm's way of foxes. Sometimes when the wind blew, especially in the winter, I'd see them huddled together on a branch, clinging on as the tree swayed to and fro. The goats were easier to look after and provided us with plenty of fresh and safe milk.

Then there were the dogs. No Romani person would allow a *juk* into their tent or wagon – our rules meant they had to live outside – so we made kennels for them from old planks of wood that people threw away or we'd weave them from willow and put a bit of tarpaulin on the top to make them waterproof. We rarely got attached to one animal as we all shared them. Our dogs were not only good at guarding us, but they also kept us fed by catching wild rabbits and dealt with any vermin that might try and wander into our camp. My dad had a special favourite – his lurcher Queenie, who regularly had pups that were much sought after and always brought a good price.

My dad liked dogs almost as much as he liked horses and believed that his dogs were the best in the North. He was competitive and always keen to prove it, and as a result we'd often go to watch our dogs race others.

All this made for a busy and interesting life and we were never bored. When we had some free time, we liked to play games. We Travellers had our own sports, like *quoits* — a game where we threw horseshoes towards a metal spike, the aim being to get them to hook on to it, which took a lot of skill. We also played *toss ha'penny,* where you threw a coin towards a wall or a piece of board and the nearest won the other players' coins. My mam frowned on this game because it was gambling. She told me a story about a Traveller boy getting lifted by the police as a warning.

When we got together with the rest of our family and other Travellers at fairs, we boys would sometimes have running races against horses. Sometimes we'd ride the horses and try to knock each other off, like old knights.

One of my favourite things about our life were the nights when we would sit around the fire and tell stories. This didn't happen so much in the winter, but when the spring came again and we went travelling, we'd end up doing it most nights. I thought I was the luckiest boy in the world as I basked in the love of my family and the light and heat of the flames.

My Uncle Billy was famous for his funny stories and songs. He could take the most ordinary things and make them so funny that your sides would hurt with laughing. He could have been one of those comedians if he'd have wanted to. Whenever he finished one story, we asked him for another one straight away.

"Hey, I need to wet my whistle," he'd say. Then he'd take a sip from a bottle of beer while someone else would have their turn.

My mam was a singer and I'd grown up with her beautiful voice. She sang to us as babies and she'd sing all the time when she was doing her work around the camp, especially on a Sunday when she sang hymns. My favourite hymn was 'Amazing Grace'. She was religious, my mam, and getting more so as time went on. "You should be in the music hall with a voice like that!" I heard a *Gorja* person say, more than once after church.

My mam would look at them disapprovingly and say, "My voice is for my family and the Lord." She had a very low opinion of the music halls and those who went to them.

We always had to make space for our *phuri dai*, who would give us a history lesson. She'd start off with, "You need to know this…" Every time we learned something new about our family and the ancient people we were connected to.

"We Romanis were here before any houses or factories. We were here when Henry VIII was king, back when they called us Egyptians, instead of Romanichals, which is our proper name."

Our grandma knew our history better than anyone, but as our Uncle Billy kept reminding us, we were living in the modern age now. The age of King George V; the age of wonder. He'd heard that in London they even had a train that went underground like a mole. My father wasn't as excited about living in the modern age. He was always wondering how long it would be before there was no space left for Romani people.

Our *phuri dai* would wave her hand as if she was waving the future away. "You have to know where you come from otherwise you won't know where yer goin'." And then she'd tell us a story we never got tired of hearing, about a Gypsy queen and a famous writer who had travelled with our people.

"Imagine that," she'd say with a wink and a smile. "A real Gypsy queen *Gorja* people would have had to bow down to and say 'yes, Your Majesty; no, Your Majesty,' to and do her bidding." Then she'd break into peals of laughter, which we would join in with, our imaginations full of people lining the streets for the Gypsy queen like they used to for Queen Victoria.

We knew that every important woman in a Romani family was classed as a queen, especially if she had a large funeral, but it was still fun to pretend there had been a real Gypsy queen. There was even a headstone with 'Gypsy Queen' on it in a graveyard in Sheffield for everyone to see.

Four

Over the next few days, my mam and dad continued to argue about me going to school, but as usual my mam had her way. I had to go. I'd been to a few schools before, so I knew enough to know that I wouldn't like it and I would probably get some trouble from the *Gorja* boys.

Henry was now old enough that he didn't have to go, but he volunteered to walk me there on my first day. As we set off towards the school, Henry must have picked up on the sense of dread and nerves I was feeling.

"It might be a good place, Lijah. Teach yer a few handy things. The world is changing. Uncle Billy's always saying we're gonna need *Gorja* learning."

I knew he was right and I wanted to learn, but I also knew I was so far behind that I'd most likely end up looking stupid. I immediately felt sick at the thought. Henry held my arm for support — but also because he knew I was ready to run off.

"Think of our mam," he said. I nodded, took a deep breath and walked forward. We were soon at the school gates. In the yard, a group of boys were kicking and chasing after a ball. There seemed to be two teams, each trying to guide the ball to the opposite side of the yard. Henry looked at me and smiled at my bemusement. "It's called football."

"Have you ever played it?" I asked, keeping my eye on the ball as it was passed from boy to boy.

"Aye, a few times, but it's not much of a game," Henry said.

The biggest boy seemed to take exception to us watching him.

"What yer lookin' at?" he called to us. "Never seen a ball before?" The other boys looked over and laughed. Henry gave him a stern look. The boys quickly stopped laughing and carried on with their game. Henry was a quiet lad – "too quiet", my uncle would often say – but my brother was as strong as an ox and brave with it.

"I've gotta go," Henry said giving my arm a squeeze and walking away, leaving me alone to face the boys.

As soon as Henry was out of sight, the big lad stopped the game, picked up the ball and came over to meet me as I walked through the gate. He stood, blocking my way into the yard.

"I know you," he said, smiling. He looked towards the other boys before turning back to me. "Yer one of them tramps that picks up other people's rubbish. I seen yer on yer cart, like a load of crows." This brought about a series of nudges, winks and sniggering behind their hands done on purpose to get a rise out of me and it worked because I felt my blood boiling. I was just about to go for him, when a stern-looking thin-faced man came out of the front door of the school, carrying a cane in one hand. After checking the time on his pocket watch, he pulled a cord that was attached to a big bell above the school's entrance, which rang out loudly.

The boys stopped their games and lined up. He nodded to each one as they walked into school. Soon there was only me left. When I got to the door, the man held his hand up to stop me and looked me over like you would an animal you were thinking of buying.

"I know who you are and where you're from and how to deal with the likes of you," he said, as he lifted up the cane he'd been leaning on. His words sent a shiver down my spine, but I knew that if he hit us for no reason my mam would be up to see him.

"I'd swing for anyone who harms my *chavvies*," was one of her usual sayings – a threat I'd seen her ready to back up on more than one occasion.

23

Henry had warned me this might happen, and that the schoolmaster would look for head lice and check whether our mother was looking after us properly.

Once in the classroom, the woman teacher made me sit away from the other children on a separate bare desk. She started talking about something and writing notes on a chalkboard behind her. None of it made much sense to me as I could hardly read or write. Even if I could, there would still have been no point to it as the teacher hadn't given me a slate or chalk like the other children had, so I just sat there listening, pretending to be interested.

About an hour and a half later, the teacher told us it was playtime and the children filed silently out of the classroom into the schoolyards, the girls one way and the boys another. Once in the boys' yard, I could see over the wall that several of the girls were starting to jump with skipping ropes. In the boys' yard, I just stood and watched the other children. Some of them were running around after each other playing tig, some were having piggyback races. Everyone seemed to have someone to talk to or play with, I just stood watching and wishing I was back at the camp.

The big lad with the football came out and the same group of boys I'd seen playing football earlier continued their game. It fascinated me how one of them could run with the ball and keep it at their feet and then just like magic another player could take it away from them with his feet and go on to score a goal.

I wanted to join in, but I knew they weren't going to ask me to.

When playtime was over, we filed back into the classroom. I watched as the teacher rubbed off what she had written on the board that morning and wrote new words. I sat in silence again, with nothing to do but think about football – the only thing that had interested me about this school so far. It seemed to take an age before it was dinner time. I sat on my own and tucked into what *habben* my mam had packed for me in brown paper. Even though the food was tasty, my mind was on one thing: having a go at that football game.

Out in the yard again, I watched the boy with the ball picking teams and organizing the game. At first, they were all looking at me, but after a while they seemed to forget I was there. My fascination with how this game worked continued: the passing, the tackling and how when you scored goal the other boys on your team shook hands with you and slapped you on the back.

When the bell went again, the boy picked up his

ball and deliberately pushed into me as I tried to go past. I balled my fists, but I knew I couldn't cause any trouble as it would come back on my family. One of the boys hung back as the others went in, sidling up to me after they had all gone.

"A word of warning," he said in a low voice, with an accent that sounded like some of the Irish Travelling people who came over to the fairs in the summer. "Don't get on the wrong side of Joe. He'll hurt yer."

I didn't know how to answer this. I knew that our Henry would make Joe sorry if he did, but I also knew that I had to fight my own battles, so I just said, "Aye, thanks," to acknowledge his warning and thank him for it.

At the end of the school day, I walked back to the camp on my own, thinking about Joe the bully and how I'd like to knock the smile right off his face. My dad was still out working with Henry, but my mam was waiting for me. She handed me a cup of tea.

"I hope your day was better than mine," she said. "I must have *hawked* fifty houses and all I got was enough to buy a bit of flour to make some bread. I hope yer dad brings some money back so we can have a bit o' butter on it."

Even though my day had been terrible, I didn't

want to tell her. I knew it would be the last thing she'd want to hear. "It was all right," I said. We both left it at that.

When my dad got home, she repeated what I'd said about school and added a bit more about how I was better off there for the time being. My dad shook his head in resignation. We had our tea and then me and Henry did all the jobs we usually did, feeding the horses and other animals and getting the cart ready for the next day. He never asked me about school, and I never told him.

I was still angry about what had happened though. My thoughts that night as I went to sleep were split between how I'd wipe the smile off Joe's face and how I could get the boys to let me play football with them. I was old enough to sort things out on my own now and that's what I was going to do.

Five

Over the next couple of weeks, I got into the routine of going to school. I wasn't learning much, apart from some new words, but at least, after that first day, I had been given a slate and chalk so I could copy some of the letters and practise writing my name. Uncle Billy had told us that we'd all need to be able to do that in the future, because everyone would have papers to fill in. Henry could already read and write properly, but he'd always been better at school than me. He could have been a good scholar if he'd have had the chance.

When I wasn't practising the letters and numbers, then I was half listening to the teacher and half thinking about football, playing over in my mind what I'd seen the boys do. I still didn't have any friends. I'd caught the Irish lad, Samuel, smiling and nodding at me a couple of times. He never spoke to me though and I reckoned it was because he was scared of Joe.

I went to school, I came back to the camp, I saw to the animals, then went to bed: the same thing, day after day. It was tiring me out. I wondered how *Gorja* people who worked in the factories and mills did it week in, week out, until they were old people. At least I'd be free of school as soon as we started travelling again.

I looked forward to my Saturdays and Sundays as even going to church with my mam was better than being in school. Since watching the boys at school play football, I'd started to notice it all over the place. When we were out collecting, boys were playing the game on any piece of grass between the terraced houses, or even in the streets. Once my dad had to pull the horse up quick and duck when a ball came flying over the cart. He shouted at the boys, and they just laughed and ran away. "*Dinlos*' game," my dad said as we carried on our way.

I even made the mistake of mentioning it to my dad, to see if he'd ever played it. He laughed, but then turned serious. "It's a daft *Gorja* game," he said firmly. "Stay away from it."

I didn't answer and certainly didn't tell him it was the main thing on my mind.

Most of the talk on the camp was about someone known as the Gypsy preacher who was coming up to Sheffield. It seemed like all my mam could talk about – my Uncle Billy and Auntie Britti too.

According to them, the preacher was famous among Travelling people and *Gorjas* in the south. He was coming up to preach nearby and this might be our only chance to see him.

My dad wasn't convinced. "I can't see it myself. Someone calling himself a Gypsy man being allowed to be a preacher. Who'd let him have a church?"

My mam was straight back at him. "The lord has called him an' doesn't mind if he calls himself a Gypsy – an' he doesn't have a church, he preaches outside. We're all goin' to see him, an' you can come with us an' see for yerself."

"Somebody has to stay here to look after everything," my dad replied. We all knew then that my dad wasn't going to be going with us, even if he could. My mam didn't seem bothered.

The day before the preacher arrived, after we'd been out *tattin* and unloaded the cart, my dad told me to get it cleaned up ready for tomorrow. "You can drive it, Lijah," he said.

The next morning, my mam made sure we were all dressed up in the best clothes we had. Uncle Billy had already decreed by looking at the sky that morning that it wouldn't rain, although it would probably stay cold. Wrapped up warm in our overcoats, we waved goodbye to my dad and set off in good time towards

31

the park. We skirted around the city — it was quiet, being a Sunday. A lot of people were in church or still at home having their breakfasts. We passed a number of lads playing football in parks and greens along the way and I tried not to stare too eagerly. An hour and a half later, we were about a quarter of a mile away. It started to get busy with more horses and carts: most were little gig carts but there were some rich people out in their grand carriages, driven by their servants.

We could hear the noise of a lot of people as we pulled up at the gates of the park. Uncle Billy and I tied the horses up together and gave them each a nose bag with chopped-up hay in it. We followed a lot of other people as we all walked towards the noise, then saw a crowd as big as the ones at a fair. There were more *Gorjas* than Romani people. At the front of the crowd, on a raised stage, stood the preacher. A tall man with a big moustache, he was standing up straight like an army colonel.

The preacher did get us to listen to him. Unlike some of the church services I'd been to, the time went quickly because he told stories just like my uncle did. There was one about someone called David and a giant called Goliath; he made it feel like you were there with them. At the end of his sermon, a lot of people left but many of the Romani people, including my mam, Auntie Britti and Uncle Billy stood in line waiting to talk to him. I heard my Uncle Billy speak in our language and when the preacher answered him back in Romani, my uncle shook the preacher's hand enthusiastically. I saw my mam smile and say to my auntie, "The *mush* can *rokker Rumness*."

While I waited for my mam to finish talking to the preacher, I was thinking about how big the crowd had been earlier and how I was sure I'd caught a glimpse of Samuel from school. Maybe it was my mind playing tricks on me.

As soon as we got back to the camp, my mam relayed the whole experience to my dad. She told him how the preacher had understood and spoke to us in our language. With the testimony of Uncle Billy, my dad finally believed that the preacher was a Romani. My dad had done all the chores while we'd been out. All that was left to do for the day was to put the carts away and feed the horses, and for us to have something to eat and go to bed.

On Monday morning at school, I was still curious to know if Samuel had been at the same preacher event as me, but I never got the chance to ask him. As I walked into the yard, he was deep in conversation with a couple of boys I hadn't seen before. One of them had a football tucked tightly under his arm. The bell rang and we all walked in silently as usual. We settled down at our desks and got on with the tasks we were given.

At playtime, Samuel and the new boys, who it turned out were his cousins, quickly organized a game of their own separate to Joe's. Every boy apart from me was involved in one of the games.

Joe seemed quieter than usual. For once, he wasn't giving me funny looks, which was just as well as I was getting to the end of my tether with him. Next stop would be a fight and all the trouble that would bring to my family.

I stood in my usual place next to the wall that divided the boys and girls' yards and watched the two games taking place. Slowly and without any organizing, the two separate games became one, with seven or eight lads on each side. Now everyone was taking it more seriously and even though I was the only boy not playing it was still interesting to watch.

The game was in full flow – boys shouting to each other to pass the ball, concentrating on kicking it towards the goals, the posts marked out by jumpers and scarves, the goalkeeper fearful of the hard leather ball hitting them. One of the lads kicked the ball high in the air. It landed near me and slowly rolled towards my feet.

34

"Kick it back then — if yer can," Joe shouted, laughing.

I didn't have to think twice about it. All that anger, all that standing by itching to play … it all went into my kick. I watched in delight as the ball took off like a cannonball heading straight for Joe — who had to duck — and carried on. It whistled past the goalkeeper.

There was a stunned silence followed by a round of applause. Samuel ran over to shake my hand. One of the new lads came up behind him.

"What a shot," he said, grinning. "You're on our team now."

Joe was scowling but there was nothing he could do. All my frustration and anger about school and Joe seem to slowly release as I focused on the game, trying to remember everything I'd seen and heard about it: tackling, keeping the ball away from other players, passing to someone on your side and then scoring a goal. Buoyed by the applause of my new teammates I was running, tackling, passing the ball. Every time Joe or one of his team tried to get the ball off me, I was determined to keep it. I was too quick for him and them and they were getting more frustrated and falling out with each other. My revenge was complete when I scored a second goal and then a third.

We won the match easily. After the game, my team

patted me on the back and shook my hand. "You got yer hat-trick!" Samuel shouted, almost as excited as I was. Even back in class, the good feeling continued. The boys who were on my team were now friendly towards me; one of them offered to loan me a pencil and to help me with my reading. As I left school and headed in the direction of our camp, Samuel's cousin George shouted over to me. "Same thing tomorrow, eh?"

I nodded and walked home replaying the game over in my mind, feeling like I was walking on air.

My dad noticed my good mood as I set to my chores. He smiled and patted me on the back.

"I know you don't like school, son, but it's good that yer putting a brave face on it for yer mam. She does worry about yer."

"Aye, Dad, I know. There's no need to though, school's all right. An' I have got better at me readin' and writin'," I replied.

My dad looked at me like he wasn't convinced. "I think Queenie's in pup, so that'll be summat to look forward to. An' we'll be on the road again before you know it."

Later, we all sat having our food around the fire. "Turnin' into a proper scholar is our Lijah," my dad said, for the benefit of my mam. "Tellin' me today he was learning more words and writin', ain't that right, son?"

"Aye, Dad, it was a good day for sure," I said truthfully, as a wide smile appeared on my mam's face.

Before I went to bed, I told Henry all about the game and how much I'd enjoyed playing. I told him at least twice about the goals I scored.

"I'm pleased for you, Lijah," he said with a serious edge to his voice. "But don't get too fond of it, because you know our dad hates the game."

I nodded, but I knew that the only thing on my mind that night would be getting to school the next day to play football.

Six

On Monday morning, my new team were waiting for me. We spent the time in the schoolyard planning the game we would play at dinnertime. I didn't score any goals, but I did help to keep the ball from Joe which stopped him scoring so we still won.

For the next two weeks, my life was all about football. I couldn't wait to get to school to play it. I felt happier than I had done for a long time. Even my dad noticed it.

"Why are you so happy?" he asked jokingly one evening.

Despite knowing that it might not go down too well with my dad I couldn't keep it bottled up any longer. The Gypsy preacher had said something about lies eating away at you and he was right. I had to tell my dad the truth. He'd be madder if he caught me playing it and I knew I couldn't stop… "I'm in a football team at school. I'm good at it," I blurted out.

His smile quickly turned to a frown, "I thought I said I didn't want yer playing that *Gorja* game?"

"I know," I answered. "But it's actually really exciting. See, there are two teams and—"

"I know how the game is played, Lijah."

Dad's voice had gone all sharp, but I wanted to make him understand.

"To start with the *Gorja* boys wouldn't let me play, but then I scored this amazing goal from across the yard and—"

But my dad had had enough.

"Quicker we get yer out of that school the better. I don't want to hear any more about that daft football, d'yer hear!"

I just nodded, hanging my head and trying to stop tears coming to my eyes. I didn't know why it had upset me so much; Henry had warned me, after all.

"I want yer to help me with the racin' horse we're gonna get. I need yer to get yer mind on that, not a *chavvies*' game. Yer need to be more like yer brother. Yer need to grow up, son."

Despite my dad's warning, I didn't stop playing football. It was easy at first to separate my life at school and my life at home, but the more I played the game, the more I wanted to be able to practise in

40

the evenings and on the weekends. If I was going to get better, I would need a leather football. I had no money, however, and I didn't dare ask my dad for any, so instead I set about making one out of rags. One afternoon, I took some of the old cloth that we called *shoddy*. It was going to be sold to be used as stuffing for furniture or made into new cloth, but it wasn't worth much, so I knew my dad wouldn't miss it. I took strip after strip, wound it tight and tied it, building up layer after layer, until I had a hard cloth ball almost the size of a leather one.

Telling everyone I was going to collect firewood for the stoves in the wagons, I picked up a basket, slipped my rag ball into it and headed to the woods. Placing the basket on the ground, I spent the next ten minutes scouring the woodland floor for dry windfall sticks, breaking them to size and putting them in the basket. That job done, I turned my attention to the ball and the trees that surrounded me. In my mind I no longer saw them as trees; they were now a team of giant players, standing strong, determined to stop me from scoring a goal.

I thought of the Bible story the preacher had told us about the giant Goliath. Now in those woods, I was David, and the trees were giants out to get me. I set off at a furious pace. I swerved around each tree, avoiding the roots trying to trip me up and take my ball off me. I made sure to keep it at my feet, even bouncing it off the trunks and getting it back under my control. Once past them, all I had to do was complete the challenge of getting the ball into a tree with a hole in it.

I stopped and focused on the hole, which was about the size of a small cartwheel. I took aim and kicked. The ball hit close to the edge of the hole. I had missed, but I was getting better and next time it would go in.

I carried the basket back to the camp with the now damp and worse-for-wear rag ball hidden under the firewood. Henry met me with a big smile on his face. "I know you've got a ball in the bottom of that basket."

"How?" I said, worried that someone else might have noticed it.

"I came up to the woods looking and I saw you kicking it at the trees. You looked like you were in a trance, so I thought it best to leave you – don't worry; your secret's safe with me," he said.

One afternoon after school, Henry beckoned me over to one of the wagons. He pointed down at my feet. "Look at the state of your boots," he said in a low voice. "Dad's gonna go *radge* if he sees them."

"I'll get some polish on them quick. He won't notice," I said.

Henry pointed to the large metal hub in the middle of one of the wagon's wheels.

"Put your foot up there," he said.

I did as he asked and he gave it a closer look, running his fingers over the toe of my boot. "The leather's gone right through; polish ain't gonna fix that," he said, shaking his head.

"What am I goin' to do?" I said, now worried. My boots were only a couple of months old and usually they'd last at least four or five months before they had to have a new sole and heel on them, but I'd never kicked the toes out before.

"Let me think," Henry said.

"Can you take them to the cobbler to be fixed?" I asked in desperation, knowing from our rag-and-bone collecting that they were probably only good for throwing away.

"Aw, Lijah, they're only a few months old an' all," Henry said, rubbing his forehead.

We both knew the importance our dad placed on a good pair of boots. We always had to have a particular type of boot: brown leather, strong stitching and fastened up the side.

"Smart and strong," my dad would say.

"Look, our dad has been letting me keep a little bit of the money from the *tattin*. I've been putting it away for when I get married in the future. I'll use some of that an' get you a new pair. We're going to have to lie to our dad and mam though, and I'm not happy about that."

"I'm sorry ... I didn't think this would happen," I said.

"You're just lucky tomorrow's Saturday and you've got such a nice big *phrala*," he said, smiling, which helped me feel a little better.

The next day, Henry put his plan into action. He persuaded our dad to let us go out *tattin* on the cart together, while he stayed on the camp making sweeping brooms. Henry and I had never worked so hard, nor called at so many houses. We had the cart full in record time, then it was off to the cobbler. It had to be a different cobbler to our usual one for Henry's plan to work or else our dad would find out.

We pushed open the door of the shop, which set off a loud bell. The shop was full of the smell of leather and glue and the noise of hammering. The cobbler, an older man with grey hair and black metal spectacles, wearing a heavy leather apron, came in from the workshop at the back.

"Afternoon. What can I do for you young fellas?" he said.

"I don't suppose you could repair them, could you?" Henry asked, pointing to my boots.

I lifted my boot up so the cobbler could have a closer look. He shook his head, confirming what we already knew.

"Looks like somebody plays football, eh? Lots of you young 'uns are ruining your boots with it. Plenty of fathers and mothers complaining."

"How much for a new pair?" Henry asked.

The cobbler pointed up to a shelf which held a selection of boots, the cheapest of which were twice the money that Henry had brought.

"Have you anything cheaper?" asked Henry.

"I've these ... I've put steel tips on the front edges – he'll not kick the toes out or wear them out in a hurry," the cobbler said, pointing to some black boots I'd seen worn by those who worked down coal mines. I immediately thought how good they would be for playing football.

I could tell by his face that Henry wasn't keen on me having them. I knew he was worried what my dad would say if we went home with a pair like that.

"Get plenty of dubbin on them and they'll turn the water as good as wellington boots," the cobbler said, clearly keen to make a sale.

"These are *kushti*, Henry," I said in a low voice. "And they're a lot less *lovver* than the others."

Henry sighed, nodded and bargained with the cobbler for the best price and handed over the money. I walked out with a new pair of boots on my feet and my old ones wrapped in brown paper.

"Thanks, Henry," I said as we made our way back on the full cart to our camp.

"Don't thank me yet. We've got to get this past our dad and that's not gonna be easy. I'm still not happy about having to lie – I hope your football playing is worth it."

Henry filled me in on what I had to do. I didn't like lying either, but I didn't want to get into big trouble. Back on the camp, my dad was pleased with the haul we'd collected.

"That's my lads! Proper Travellers," he said, rubbing his hands together and looking over what we'd brought back, calculating the sizeable sum it was going to bring in.

"We had a bit of trouble though," Henry said. I held my breath. "Lijah was helping me to lift that bit of iron and we dropped it, and it ripped the front of his boot. It's all right though, because an old widow in one of the houses gave us a nearly new pair. Must have been her late husband's."

My dad looked down at my new boots which, as instructed by Henry, I'd roughed up a bit and smeared some mud on. "Them's not Traveller boots. You look like a collier," he said disapprovingly.

"Aye, I know, Dad," Henry said quickly. "But he can wear them to school and when we're out working, and he can get the others stitched up and keep them for best. Me mam'll be happy that his feet are safe, and they've cost us nowt."

Henry's words seemed to have done their job. My dad, now satisfied, nodded his head. I put my old boots away in my tent, still wrapped in the brown paper – our secret safe for now.

That night before bed I thanked Henry for the twentieth time. Looking at my new boots, he smiled and said, "Let's hope our dad doesn't work it all out, eh."

I did feel bad for what I'd done and for making Henry lie for me, but that feeling was soon replaced with one of anticipation for how these boots might improve my game. And improve it they did. Not only could I kick the ball harder and further, but they also protected my ankles from the other boys' kicks and made me more confident. I loved those boots and polished them every night.

"I've never seen a *chavvi* look after a pair of boots like him," my dad said to my mam, as he watched me shine them.

"He's a good lad," my mam said. "He knows that widow gave him her husband's boots and he's doing what the Lord says about repaying her kindness."

My dad just nodded and walked away. I turned my head so my mam wouldn't see the shame on my face. But even that shame wasn't enough to make me think about giving up football.

Seven

It was Sunday afternoon. The sun was hanging low in the late winter sky, but there was still a bit of warmth in it and my dad had a job for us.

"You and Henry harness Bessie and see how she runs now," he said. Bessie was a young pony we'd bred ourselves. We'd been training her in the cart, but she'd picked up a little bit of a limp, so my father had been working on her foot with some of the old medicine that my *phuri dai* had shown him how to make. It was mainly boiled up roots of nettles, which we had bathed her leg with over the past three days.

Henry and me were only too happy to take her out for a run, to see if our animal husbandry had paid off. We harnessed her, backed her into the shafts, fixed the traces to the cart then climbed on and turned her towards the road.

"Don't race 'er," my father shouted after us, which made us both laugh because he talked so much about getting a cart-racing horse, but we knew those were a different breed. He was warning us not to cause injury to the pony, which he was hoping to sell. He needn't have worried though – we didn't want that either. We loved that little pony and would be sorry to see her go.

We knew why he'd warned us though. Sometimes when Travelling people saw each other out with their horses and carts, there'd be an element of competition between them as to who had the fastest horse and they'd race them against each other along the road. It was dangerous for a number of reasons. With so much traffic in a city like Sheffield, you could collide with a tram or another cart. And, if they saw you, you'd get in trouble with the police and then again with your father when you got home.

I took the reins and gently urged Bessie in the direction of Owlerton. We looped at a nice gentle trot around the stadium. Henry knew why I'd come out this way. I pulled Bessie and the cart to a stop to have a look at the stadium. Just for a moment, I allowed myself to daydream about being inside it, watching the football. I wondered what it would be like to play on a proper field.

"Lijah," Henry said, tugging on my arm. "We need to get on."

I gently slapped the reins on Bessie's rump and said, "Git up!" Slowly, we moved forward, away from

50

the stadium. I urged her to pick up a bit of speed as we turned on to a nice level bit of road, where I pushed her on faster for a few minutes and then slowed her down as a group of older lads playing a game of football caught my attention. I pulled Bessie up near the edge of the green they were playing on, gave the reins to Henry and jumped off to take a closer look.

"Lijah! What're you doing?" he said in surprise as he took the reins. The lads stopped playing and came over to us.

I felt the air of hostility as they came within touching distance.

"Yer Gypsies, int yer?" the biggest one said with a snarl, his unkempt blond hair blowing across his face.

I couldn't help myself – as big as he was, I wasn't going to be spoken to like that by anyone.

Pulling myself up to my full height I replied, "Aye, and what of it?"

Henry, ever the peacemaker, quick as a flash tried to calm things.

"What rules do you play?" he asked.

This broke the tension and the lad, an obvious modern football fan, proudly told Henry that they were playing FA rules. However, it was clear that wasn't enough to put right what I had started.

"Does this little 'un play? If he can play as well as

he uses his mouth, he'll be good," the big blond-haired lad said, as the others backed him up with laughter.

I could see his idea was to teach me a lesson; it was a chance for him and his friends to rough me up without being seen as bullies.

"I'll play," I said, full of confidence.

"Lijah, no," Henry said, putting his hand on my shoulder to hold me back.

"He'll be safe wi' us. We won't be playing Sheffield rules, will we, Arthur?" another lad said, with a wink at his blond friend.

"Nah, course not, Lenny," he replied winking back at him. One of the many things I had learned from playing with the lads at school was about the different rules in football, but I knew by the way he said it, we weren't going to be playing by any fair rules.

"You can have him on your side," the one called Lenny said, I guessed this was because he wanted to have a go at me which suited me fine because that gave me the opportunity to have a go at him. I could see from the worried expression on my brother's face that he didn't share my enthusiasm for being a part of this game, but, knowing that he couldn't stop me, pulled me to him and said, "Lijah, be very careful."

"They've picked on the wrong Gypsy this time," I said.

Henry just shook his head.

As soon as the game kicked off, I could tell it was going to be a rough one. I knew what Sheffield rules were – they were old ones that meant you could barge into people and pick up the ball as well. I managed to get the ball to my feet fairly quickly and had a little inward chuckle as I saw the look of surprise on the face of the boy who'd just lost it. Then the fun started. I ran with the ball towards the goal. Two of the opposing players came at me and I felt the anger and power rise within me. I sent them flying as I ran between them and kept running until the ball went past the lad acting as the goalkeeper.

There was no handshake or other sign of appreciation for what I'd done; instead, they really had it in for me. Every time I had the ball, I was shoved off it, my feet were stamped on, my shins and ankles kicked, even my face took a couple of elbow blows. But I was enjoying myself and I ran and ran round them, until they were tired out. My new boots protected my ankles from the worst of it, but I was marked pretty much everywhere else.

Eventually, the big lad Arthur called the end of the game and I walked back towards where Henry was waiting for me.

"Hey, little Gypsy," one of the lads called. "You're not a bad player. Come back sometime."

"My name is Lijah Vesh, not what you called me,"
I said angrily. I raised my fists, ready to go for him.

I felt Henry's arms around me, holding me back
as he whispered in my ear, "Don't, Lijah. Not here."

"Whoa, I was only having a bit of fun wi' yer," the
lad said, moving away from us.

Henry, still with one arm around me, steered me
back to the cart.

"Yer going to have to be careful, Lijah, they could
have mullered us," he said when we were safely away.

"I'd have mullered him first," I said sullenly. "I'm
fed up with it, Henry. People looking down on us all
the time."

"We're Romanis. You can't change that, and you
will never stop them calling us names," he said.

"I don't want to change what I am. I want them
to change how they talk about us. You watch, Henry,
one day when I'm a famous footballer, people like him
will be calling me Mr Vesh."

Henry laughed and, after a moment, I laughed
along with him.

"We'd better get you cleaned up as best we can,
Lijah, and then get home. Our dad will be wondering
where we are."

We stopped at a horse trough at the side of the
road. Using the water and a piece of rag off the cart,

Henry cleaned me up as well as he could. There was nothing he could do about the rip in my trousers or the tear in the sleeve of my jersey, though.

My dad watched us drive the cart back into our camp, paying close attention to how Bessie walked. When we stopped and got off the cart, my dad looked at the big lump on my forehead, the cut above my left eye and the swelling around the right one.

"Did yer give a good account of yerself? Did yer win?"

I nodded yes to both questions, which was true, but I wasn't being totally honest as I knew my father thought I'd been in a fist fight, not a football game.

"Who was it?"

"*Gorja* boys," Henry said quickly.

My dad smiled and slapped me on the back. "*Kushti*, proper little boxing *mush*, eh?" he said, pleased that I'd won a fight and that I hadn't caused a rift with another Traveller family.

I enjoyed the praise from him even though it made me feel guilty. That night, as I lay in my bed with some of my mam's lavender ointment on my cuts and bruises, feeling the tightening and ache of my muscles, I couldn't stop thinking about the game of football and how it had made me feel. I wasn't just a small Gypsy on that field. I was powerful and free.

56

Eight

Our camp, like others around the city, was a safe place for the winter, but as soon as spring came and the weather was good enough, we'd be off travelling, finding new customers for all the things we made and catching up with relatives who we may not have seen for many months or even a whole year. Then there were the horse fairs: places to sell our horses, make some money and have some fun. And for the older boys and girls, the fairs were the best places to meet a future wife or husband.

My dad would decide when spring officially started.

"Smell that," he said on one particular morning, standing like an army general and sniffing the air. "Winter is losing its grip." He never had a calendar or watch – he claimed he didn't need one. "Them things are just for people who are ruled by time. We aren't."

My dad's declaration meant that we had to pack everything down ready for travel. The wagons had to have their wheels and all their moving parts greased. Harnesses were checked and repaired where needed and the site had to be left clean and tidy.

We were soon ready to set off on our travels. I was looking forward to the journey. It would be good to see new places and meet new people. The weather was warming up and the wild foods would be plentiful. We'd still have to worry about the police moving us on, but at least we didn't have to go to school. None of us liked school.

This year, however, was different for me. As much as I was keen to get away from school, I was going to miss playing football with the lads there. I might even miss the lessons a bit. They were still hard, but with the help of some of the lads when the teacher wasn't looking, I was getting better at reading and writing and arithmetic.

Leaving Sheffield meant that we'd be able to see some different places and meet up with lots of our relatives. Every year there were new baby cousins that our aunties wanted us to coo and fuss over, and our uncles were desperate to show off their horses and dogs at the horse fairs.

It was grand to be on the road, sat on the flat cart or walking along beside it, the big wagon following behind us and another flat cart behind that. On a good day, we'd do between ten to fifteen miles. It kept us fit, that was for sure, and I believe it was the best training I could have had for what I came to think of as my passion, my sport. The wind on my face, the sound of the horses' hooves, the creaking and jingle of the leather harnesses and the trundling of the big metal-rimmed cartwheels made me feel I was not only free, but part of a big musical machine.

Spring was a good time of year to start making money. When we found a good place to stop, every camp became a hive of activity. Food was cooked, wooden items made, babies tended to, animals checked and fed, clothes washed and hung out to dry, and carts fixed. We were like a small mobile family factory, taking the raw materials from the woods and turning them into products that we could sell: clothes pegs, sweeping brooms, clothes line props and even wooden toys for children. All Traveller children were very skilled at making clothes pegs and other wooden items, like spoons and stools. We'd built up a stock of them during the winter and looked forward to selling them as we travelled and then making more as we needed. The spring and summer willow and hazel wood was always easier to work with when the sap had risen.

Then there were the piles of old clothes and scrap

that we'd collected, which needed sorting through to see what was to be sold on and what was to be kept for ourselves. The anticipation of who would join us as we travelled and who we would meet at a fair or big stopping place was all part and parcel of the fun.

One family, who usually stopped on the Derbyshire side of Sheffield, always tried to meet up with us on the road and then travel with us to one of the fairs. We might not have seen them for six months or more, but within ten minutes we were all sitting around talking, eating and playing like one big family.

They had a son called Thomas, who was a year or so younger than me, and a daughter called Genty, who was the same age as Henry. We'd all grown up together and Genty was like a big sister to me. Me and Thomas got along well enough, even though he had no idea about football. When we were up in the woods, gathering some willow, I tried to explain the rules to him. I showed him some of my skills, kicking dry pinecones that were lying on the floor, but he didn't seem very impressed.

Genty and Henry seemed to be much better suited. When they went off together to fetch water, talking and laughing with each other, I caught my mam smiling after them.

The next day all four of us went up into the woods

to collect firewood and willow and had a *kushti* time, laughing and joking. We even took some food, which we ate sat beside a waterfall. Me and Thomas walked beside each other on the way back to the camp. He was telling me about his passion for racing horses, but I was only half listening. Behind us, I could hear Genty and Henry *rokkering* away, but couldn't make out what they were saying. I wondered how they could have so much to *rokker* about.

Sat around the fire at night, with my belly full of the most delicious food, the stories would start. I would think of myself as the luckiest boy in the world. I was free and I had parents who loved me and the animals to look after. There was only one thing that stopped it being perfect. I missed playing football. It was like my whole body, especially my legs, were pining for it.

The trade was good with the locals at the first stopping place, so we stayed until no one wanted to buy anything else, then we all moved on towards the fair. We travelled nearly every day and when we stopped, we spent a little time making things.

The women in Genty's family were known for their lacemaking, which was something I loved to watch them do. Genty, though, was the best I'd ever seen.

Watching her nimble fingers work the threads and seeing the patterns appear was magical. I could see she loved lacemaking as much as I loved football. The only difference was her skills were going to make her money. Mine wouldn't make me any unless I could be a professional footballer. I chided myself for having such a daft thought.

Her mam saw me and Henry watching her work and said proudly, "My lass is gonna be famous among Travellers for this. The man who she marries is going to have an easy life, for sure."

When we got to the fair, it was already busy; there were at least thirty wagons parked up in a number of circles with tents pitched beside and behind them. Horses were tethered and grazing on the surrounding grass. People were cooking, children were playing, and the adults were catching up with each other as well as starting to do deals. Money was changing hands for all kinds of goods. Genty's mam wasn't wrong. Her lace was sold out the first day.

My dad, trying to get me as excited about horse racing as he was, made sure we watched every race. He talked to the horse owners and tried to find the foal he was always looking for.

Try as I might, I couldn't muster much enthusiasm for horse racing. Looking at the way my dad watched them, the passion he had for every part of every race was clear for everyone to see. It dawned on me his love of horses mirrored my love of football. For the first time, I understood his passion, and wondered if he would ever understand mine.

That afternoon, my dad's long-held dream came true, when he found the perfect trotting horse to buy. The fact that it hadn't been born yet didn't deter him from doing the deal. The mare was a fine horse and the stallion they planned to breed with her was a champion. My dad shook hands with the owner, taking the chance that the next foal this pair had would be as good as its parents. That handshake meant that the deal was done. My dad would stump up half the money as soon as the foal was born and the other half when it could safely leave its mother.

That night around the fire, there were a lot of families talking, eating and enjoying themselves. My dad was in a particularly good mood, celebrating his deal with the horse. Even though it might be over a year before we had the foal, he was happy that his search was over. The atmosphere was as good as I'd ever experienced, but somehow, I didn't totally feel part of it. I went to bed early, just wishing I had someone to talk to about football.

Genty and Henry were standing in the shadows of

one of the wagons. I didn't see them at first, just heard their voices.

"There's a different life to this, you know," Genty was saying quietly.

"Aye, I know," Henry replied.

"We have to do it someday, Henry. We have to." I'd never heard Genty sound so serious.

I saw their two shadows move closer together as I walked on to my tent.

Nine

The summer had gone well for all of us. We'd made money and enjoyed ourselves with our family, and you couldn't get much better than that according to my dad. I had enjoyed it, but for the first time ever I was looking forward to getting back to Sheffield. I couldn't wait to play football again.

On the first morning I was due back at school, my dad, who had been grumbling about it all weekend, said to my mam, "Does he have to go back, Kushy? He's nearly of age now."

We could always tell when things were serious my dad always used my mam's name. My mam answered him with an edge to her voice. "Yer know he has to. Yer don't want us to get lifted by the police now, do yer?"

Reluctant to give in, my dad pushed it further. "Look at the size of him: he's nearly as big as Henry! If anybody asks, he can just give Henry's name."

My mam, as usual, had the final word. "He's going to school, Abe, and that's that."

Back at school I realized that my dad was right — the summer had done me good in terms of growing. I was now a head bigger than some of the other lads. But the first game of football showed me that I'd gone backwards as a player, messing up a couple of easy shots, and that angered me.

Back at the camp, our lives continued as usual, on the surface at least. The wagons and tents were in their usual positions, my dad and Henry carried on rag-and-bone collecting and I fed and looked after the animals when I came home from school. Whenever I could, I sneaked up to the woods to play against the trees with the rag ball.

It might have seemed the same, but things were changing. Henry was working harder than he ever had and I thought I knew why. I reckoned he and Genty had feelings for each other and that was the reason he kept trying to persuade my dad to give him more responsibilities. This made my dad praise Henry's hard work more and more. He kept making comments to me like, "As soon as you get away from that school, we'll make you a proper Romani man like our Henry."

My dad had encouraged Henry to buy his own cart, with the idea he'd go out with it one day a week and keep all the money he earned.

Henry bought an old one and we all helped him to fix it up and paint it.

I was pleased for Henry but, because he often didn't return until late in the day, it meant that more work at the camp fell on my shoulders, and this gave me less opportunity to practise my football skills. It seemed like everyone else was getting what they wanted: my dad had his horse and Henry had his cart and the independence that came with it.

I was getting fed up with having to hide my football playing from my family. I kept trying to summon up the courage to come clean about it – to tell my dad and everyone else – but always at the last minute I just couldn't bring myself to do it.

One afternoon, I was just about to offer to go up to the woods to get some firewood, when Henry came back from his first solo rag-and-bone collecting mission. By the looks of the cart, he'd had a good day. My dad looked at Henry with a sense of pride.

Henry called me over to help him unload the cart and take the horse out of the harness. By the time I'd finished unloading, it was too late to go up to the woods.

I walked towards the fire where everyone else was sitting down drinking warm tea, waiting for their food and listening to Henry tell them about his day. He took something out of a sack.

"This is for you, Lijah," he said, throwing me a worn-out looking leather ball. Without even thinking about it, I held it on my chest, dropped it on to my right foot, then tapped it upwards and passed it from foot to foot. I flicked it up on to one of my shoulders, then the other.

I suddenly realized where I was and let the ball drop, holding it still with my foot. The group of usually very noisy people sat, stunned into silence. I didn't know what to do.

My Uncle Billy came to my rescue, clapping his hands and laughing.

"Hey, look at that *mush* – he could be in a circus with them tricks," he said.

"They're not circus tricks," I said, staring hard at the ground. "It's a sport. And I'm going to be a professional footballer someday."

The words were out before I even had time to think about them.

"Put that stupid ball away and then come and say sorry to yer Uncle Billy," said my dad angrily. "And if I see that ball again it's going on the fire. An' you, Henry. What'd yer get him a ball for!

"It's only a ball. Our Lijah works as hard as anybody; I just thought he deserved a bit of fun. He shouldn't have to hide that – he's doing nothing wrong." I was so grateful to Henry for backing me.

My Uncle Billy waded in with his thoughts backing up my dad. "Both of yer should be *ladged*. Yer don't see grown men still playin' wi' hoops and tops."

I knew I'd overstepped the mark and I felt bad that Henry's kindness had got him into trouble as well. Now I was in a total bind. I wanted to share my love of football, wanted to get other people in my family interested, but all I'd done was get both Henry and me in trouble.

The next day, I tried to persuade my mam to have a word with my dad to get him to change his mind. "Just leave him for a while, Lijah," was all she said.

At least I had the leather ball. As worn as it was, it still better than the rag one I'd been playing with. And I realized what I'd said was true. Football wasn't just a game to me. I wanted it to be more than that – football was what I wanted to do with my life.

Going up to the woods became harder than ever. I wished I had someone to talk to about everything, but Henry became so busy making his own money that I hardly saw him. He'd bought his own horse and taken it over to see Genty. He brought back a piece of lace for my mam, which she had given pride of place in the wagon and told everyone about.

According to my mam, Henry was selling selected old clothes to Genty, who was using her sewing skills to turn them into new dresses and coats, then selling them on for a good profit.

"She's got a good business brain, that girl," my mam said.

"I wish we had one like her," my dad said.

I wasn't sure if he meant he wished he had a daughter like her or that he wished I had a better business brain. I honestly wished I could have been as passionate about wood carving, or horses or making money, but it just wasn't in me the way football was.

The following Sunday after we'd gone to church my mam told us to leave our best church clothes on as we were expecting a visitor. 'A gentleman parson from Rotherham way' was how she described him. I had no idea why a man like him would be coming to see us.

"Another one who just wants to find out about us, like we're wild animals in a zoo," my dad said, pulling at his stiff Sunday collar. I could tell he was desperate to spend time with the horses and his beloved dog Queenie.

"It's not like that, Abe. This man is a proper history scholar as well as a reverend. Now you all be on your best behaviour – we don't want him to think we're a bunch of heathens, do we?" she said.

"Shall I call you 'Selina ma'am' when he comes a-callin'?" my dad asked in the voice of a gentleman.

My mam laughed and shooed him away. She knew he wouldn't let her down.

Ten

My father was a dealing man. He would buy, sell or swap anything with anyone he thought he could make a profit from. That's how we lived. It was a big task for him and my mam to keep us fed and clothed and we were always aware of that. The older we got, the more we felt the responsibility, and so we were supposed to, because we knew it would be our responsibility to do it for our families when the time came.

Sometimes we made a bit of extra money from selling the pups from my dad's highly prized lurcher dog Queenie. Little did I know a buyer of one of Queenie's pups was going to change my life for ever.

"Never seen anyone work as hard as your brother," my dad said admiringly one evening, as Henry came back from rag-and-bone collecting with another large haul.

I'd only been home from school an hour and I hadn't stopped working my way through a long list of chores, not that anybody had noticed. It was true Henry was a grafter. He was fast becoming the best collector of old stuff. Even other families were noticing it. As good as it was for Henry, it meant lots more work for me. On top of it all, Queenie had given birth to a large litter of pups. I tried not to be bitter about all the extra work, but it was hard.

I helped Henry unload and stack his stuff then headed towards the fire to get a cup of tea.

"Boys," my dad said as we filled our cups from the metal pot, "there's a *mush* comin' soon for one of the pups." Henry and I looked at each other, puzzled. No one else but us had seen Queenie's new litter. The first looker always had the pick of the litter; this was usually reserved for a close relative.

"He's an important *mush*," my dad went on, "so be on your best behaviour."

My dad had us put out a couple of Windsor chairs near the fire. My mam set up a little wooden table, which she covered in a white lace cloth and laid out her best china plates and cups. These were usually only brought out for weddings and funerals when there was a celebration or a wake. I'd only seen the cups and plates used a handful of times in my life. Whoever this *mush* was, he really was getting the full family welcome.

The man arrived in a pony trap, pulled by a very nice grey. When the trap stopped, my dad beckoned Henry over.

"Take the pony and give it some water and tie it up to the old cart," he instructed.

As Henry led the horse past me, I could see that the horse, trap and leather harness were all top quality. It was clear that this man had some *wonga*. After being introduced to my mam, he and my dad sat down on their chairs and started to drink tea. We all crowded around in a circle, curious to know who he was.

"Aren't you going to introduce me to your family properly?" the man said smiling, his big voice booming around our camp.

"Aye … yes, this is Mr Davis," said my dad, looking at Mr Davis nodding and smiling, then looking at the rest of us while using his best salesperson's voice: the one he used when he was trying to get the best deal from someone. I could tell he was a bit nervous which wasn't like my dad. We knew it must have been important, so we were on our best behaviour.

"Aye, Jack Davis is my name and I'm pleased to be associated with your father."

Not everyone who was standing around watching was a child of my father, but we didn't correct the man.

Jack was a well-built man with a big stomach, a round face and a prominent nose with a big walrus moustache underneath it. When he took his hat off, there was a shock of grey hair. It was hard to work out his age compared to my father, but it was clear from his build, and the fact that his hands and fingernails showed no signs of manual labour, that he was a prosperous man and when he unbuttoned his overcoat, it revealed a gold watch and heavy chain hanging from his waistcoat.

"Nowt much better in life than horses, dogs, football and a few jars of ale with a good man like yer father," he said. He looked over to me and Henry. "Do either of you boys play football?"

I glanced at Henry. I wasn't sure what to say after my dad's outburst the other night.

To my surprise, my father enthusiastically piped up, "Oh, aye, Lijah does, Jack. Very good at it an' all. Go an' get that football of yours and show Mr Davis how good yer are."

My father gave me the eye – a signal not to question his instruction. I was confused but more than happy to go along with it. I quickly retrieved the old leather ball from my tent and proceeded to show Mr Davis what I could do.

I could tell he was impressed. "Hey, that lad of

yours knows his way around the ball, that's for sure. Do you play in a team?" he asked me.

"No, Mr Davis."

"I've seen him play, Mr Davis," Henry said, with a quick glance towards our dad. "He can take on lads twice his size and leave 'em face down in the mud."

I saw my dad's eyebrows go up in surprise. Me and Henry both knew that what had changed was not my father's opinion of football, but that he was doing business with a man he wanted to impress. Still, that was fine by me, if it meant I could talk about the game I loved without getting into any trouble.

"He should," said Mr Davis, looking back at my dad. "Football is going to be the sport of the future and the people who play it will not only be heroes but will be well compensated financially. We are fortunate, are we not, that we are in the centre of the world not only for steel but also for football?"

My father just nodded in agreement.

"You see football is not just about entertaining people. It's about keeping boys and young men fit and on the right path. Boys who play football will be healthier and stronger and we all want that, don't we?" My father nodded again as Mr Davis continued.

"You see, Abe, football will strengthen a boy's

77

body and mind. Not only will he be a better worker, he'll also be a better soldier for the next war."

My dad didn't nod or say anything in response to this. His face had gone red, and I knew he was trying to keep his anger in check. My dad did not want any of us to be workers in mills or down coal mines ... or in any job. And he certainly didn't want us to be soldiers.

Mr Davis didn't seem to notice and carried on talking, now looking directly at me.

"We'll have to talk more about football, young Lijah," he said with a smile.

All I could say to that was, "Yes, Mr Davis."

Inside I was bursting with delight that there was someone besides the boys at school who I could talk to about football.

We followed Mr Davis and my dad over to the whelping box we'd made for Queenie. She lay contentedly while the pups, with their eyes still closed, greedily fed from her.

"Which one do you reckon is the best?" Mr Davis asked, looking them over.

"They're all good, Jack. Queenie's never had a bad pup yet," my dad replied truthfully.

I reached out to move a pup that had become dislodged from its food supply.

"I'll take that one," said Mr Davis.

My dad lifted up the dark pup and handed it to Mr Davis. "This little lass is yours, Jack."

"I'll call her Bess," Mr Davis said. "After Dick Turpin's horse."

He and my dad roared with laughter. I put Bess back with her mother, wondering what was so funny about Dick Turpin's horse.

After it was agreed that he would be able to take his pup home in three weeks' time, Mr Davis said goodbye to all of us, making a point of thanking my mam for the hospitality.

"Nice to meet you, Mr Davis," I said, as politely as I could.

"Call me Jack, lad," he replied.

"He can call you Uncle Jack," my dad said quickly. Calling an older person 'Uncle' was a sign of respect in our community.

Uncle Jack climbed back into his pony trap and trotted away from the camp.

After he had gone, my dad released a sigh, like he'd been holding his breath the entire time. "He's an important man," he told us, as if we hadn't already figured that out. "We've got to keep him sweet."

"He seems to know a lot about football," my mam said, now busy cooking over the fire.

"Aye, he does and more's the pity. He's real stuck on it – pays to watch it, even talks about having his own team," my dad said, shaking his head.

"I take it he's going to be coming to the camp more?" my mam said.

"Aye, we've got some profitable business together," my dad said.

"Just make sure he knows our ways," my mam said, wielding the big wooden spoon to emphasize her point.

Later that same night, when we were alone in our tent, Henry whispered to me in the dark.

"You awake, Lijah?"

"Mmm," I replied.

"I've got something to tell you."

I thought I already knew what it was, but I waited for Henry to go on. I was guessing that he was going to ask Genty's family if he could start courting her, but he'd gone one step further than that: he had asked, and her father had said yes. Henry and Genty were officially courting.

"I wanted to tell you first, Lijah," he said. I leant over and shook his hand.

"So pleased for you, Henry," I said. I really was. I couldn't think of anyone better than Genty to have as a sister-in-law and I knew they made each other happy. As I lay in my bed though, listening to Henry's steady breathing, I got the feeling that there was something he wasn't telling me. But try as I might, I couldn't think what it could be.

Eleven

Uncle Jack became a regular visitor to our camp. I realized that, despite their differences, he and my dad had become friends as well as business associates. Uncle Jack shared my dad's love of horse racing and was prepared to go in as partners on the foal my dad had agreed to buy. They talked about it a lot, although I got the feeling that Uncle Jack's interest was more on being able to make a profit from it, rather than from having the same love of horses as my dad.

I, on the other hand, was becoming less and less interested in horses and more and more interested in football. I had a couple of conversations with Uncle Jack about the sport, out of earshot of my dad. It was clear that he had a lot to teach me about it and I was an eager pupil.

Over the next few weeks, we saw a lot more of Uncle Jack. He was a partner in an ironmonger's shop that was now stocking a lot of our pegs, brooms and other wooden items. He had contacts all over

Sheffield, including one who allowed us to take as many used hessian sacks as we could fit on the cart; these we were going to sort through, repair and sell on for a good profit. We knew for sure that Uncle Jack's support was going to play a major part in not only helping us survive the winter but to thrive through it.

Every chance I got to talk to Uncle Jack, I asked him every question I could think of about football. It seemed to me like he knew everything about it. He told me facts and figures about the players, and so many names and dates I could hardly keep them in my mind, though I remembered the Sheffield Football Association was formed before I was even born.

"You sure are keen, young man. I'm still trying to fathom how you can grow up in Sheffield and not know about football," he told me one day, after I'd asked him another burst of questions.

Careful not to say that my dad didn't want me playing or that I couldn't read the newspapers, I just said, "People like us and the people who live in houses keep away from each other."

He nodded his head like he understood, but it was clear that he didn't. Nobody could unless they lived like us. Our life was arguably harder than the *Gorja* people's lives, but we were better off in many ways, particularly regarding freedom. We had no rent to pay, we had no boss, and we could travel whenever we wanted, depending on the weather. As my *phuri dai* always reminded us, "We live in God's free air." I hadn't really understood that when I was younger but felt like I was starting to now.

Uncle Jack interrupted my thoughts.

"There's a man I need to tell you about—" he started to say, but before he could finish, my dad called me over.

"Sorry, Jack, but I need Lijah to help me with the cart," he said, giving me a look that I knew meant I should get moving, sharpish.

"I was just about to tell him about Rab How—"

"I'd rather you didn't, Jack, especially not on the camp," my dad said without any further explanation.

Uncle Jack gave him a nod. "Another time, Lijah," he said to me.

I did as I was told, but I didn't forget what Uncle Jack had started to tell me. I was desperate to find out who this Rab was, so I asked Henry later that evening.

"Don't let me mam or dad know I told yer this, Lijah, but Rab Howell was a proper footballer in Sheffield – and a Traveller. All I can tell you is that there was some trouble and he left. So just leave it be."

*

Of course, I wasn't going to let that be. I was going to find out about this man and if he really was a Traveller.

I began to wonder what exactly the trouble was that he'd been involved in and if that was the reason no one was giving me the information I wanted.

I vowed to find out more from Uncle Jack.

The next time he came up to the camp I plucked up the courage to ask him about this footballer called Rab.

It was clear that Uncle Jack was nervous talking about this on the camp: he lowered his voice and said, "Quick history of Rab Howell: born in a wagon on a camp like yours about thirty years ago. He played for United and England and was one of the best players I ever saw. I even spoke to him a few times – nice man, loved his football."

"What happened to him? Is he dead?"

"No, he got accused of cheating and he left to play for Liverpool."

I was desperate for our conversation to continue but my mam and dad were walking towards us and it was clear I was going to get no more information about Rab Howell. I was already wracking my brain for who else I could ask about him.

It didn't take me long to find out more from the boys at school; he'd been a hero to some of their dads. The next day at school as the boys stood waiting to be let in, I said to Samuel, "You ever heard of a football player called Rab Howell?"

He shook his head.

Joe piped up. "Rab Howell was my dad's favourite player; he knows everything about him."

"Who was he?" Samuel asked.

"A footballer who grew up like me and he played for England. I just want to find out more about him," I replied.

"I'll ask my dad if you want," Joe said.

I was shocked that Joe was talking to me and doubly so that he knew about Rab Howell and was willing to find out more information for me.

"Thanks!" I said.

Walking back from school that day, instead of being pleased with how my football playing had been, and how Joe had offered to help, my heart was still heavy with a problem I'd been battling with for the last few games. I needed to speak to Henry about it. As luck would have it, as I was walking into the camp, he was returning with another fully loaded cart of old stuff.

"Hey, *Phrala*," he said smiling. "Give me a hand to get this lot off, will yer?"

He stood on the cart and manoeuvred the bags of woollens and rags towards me. I placed them carefully on the ground.

"Lijah, I've got summat for yer," my dad called over from the other side of our camp. "Come and get it when you've done that."

"Yes, Dad," I replied.

I could see Henry was tired as he handed things down to me, but I needed to tell him something. "Henry I ... I don't know what to do." I saw a look of concern appear on Henry's face. "It's nowt bad," I said quickly.

"What is it then?" Henry asked.

"Football," I said. "I don't want to sound boastful, but I'm too good for them boys at school. They're no opposition for me any more. I need to play with better people, like them big lads at Owlerton. Will you tek me?"

Before Henry could answer, my dad shouted for me again. He did not like people keeping him waiting.

"Comin'," I shouted back, before whispering to Henry, "Well, will yer tek me?"

"Lijah, it's not as easy as that any more. I'm courting now," he said.

I tried not to look too disappointed and walked over to where my dad was sat with my mam. Both of them had serious looks on their faces, I immediately wondered if I was in trouble for something.

"Someone's left you a present," my dad said.

"Oh, aye," I said smiling, thinking this was some kind of joke. My dad was known to play a trick or two on us, so I kept smiling to let him know I knew what he was doing.

"He's not joshin' yer," my mam said seriously.

"Jack ... yer Uncle Jack came to take his pup and he left summat for yer." He reached a hand down to pick up a canvas bag and with the other hand he pulled out a leather football and passed it to me. I held it in my hands and silently marvelled at it, then held it to my nose and smelled it. Yes, definitely new. Not a scuff on it and already blown up — it looked like one of the latest ones too. I couldn't speak for a moment; I was so taken aback. I knew if I'd have bought a football, my dad would not have been happy, but because Uncle Jack had got it for me, that made it all right. My dad knew it would have been extremely bad form to refuse a gift from a friend. I also knew that being a dealing man, my father would want to keep Uncle Jack sweet and not spoil the deals he had going with him. Not even over a football.

"I don't want you kickin' it around the camp," he said, a note of warning in his voice.

"I won't — can you tell him thanks when you see him?"

"You can tell him yerself. He's got some old metal

things for me. I was going to get Henry to go with me tomorrow to pick them up, but you can do it instead – give Henry a rest. He's got other business to attend to."

I put the ball back in the canvas bag. As I did, I noticed a brown envelope with my name on it. I put the bag in my tent for safekeeping.

Twelve

I was desperate to try out my new football, so once my chores were done, I set off up to the common. It was the first time I could play the game I loved out in the open without fear of being seen and getting into trouble with my dad. I carried my football as carefully as you would carry a new-born *chavvi*, it was so beautiful. At first, I just wanted to admire it and not spoil its perfect looks by kicking it, but as soon as I got on to the common, with its flat close-cropped grass, the urge to play with the ball became too strong.

I gently placed it on the ground and started to tap it with my right foot, dribbling it forward further and faster, feeling the excitement and energy building, until I felt the overwhelming urge to kick it. Despite not putting my full power into the kick, my new ball soared up into the air like a bird and landed with a bounce on the grass twenty yards ahead. I was already on it before it could roll away, lining it up for another kick. I put as much power as I could into it, sending it higher than any ball I'd ever kicked before. Seeing it sail through the air was magical. I felt like I was flying with the ball.

I couldn't resist taking it into the woods and having a few shots against the trees. I got so engrossed in what I was doing that I lost track of time. It was starting to go dark, so I headed back to the camp as quickly as possible. The joy of having this new football had made me smile so much the muscles in my face were hurting.

Back at the camp, I warmed myself by the fire and drank the cup of tea my mam gave me.

"How was it?" she asked smiling.

I smiled back and nodded. I think she understood that I couldn't find the words to explain exactly how good it was.

"You'd better get to bed. Your dad'll want all the animals checked, fed and watered in the morning before you go off to the town tomorrow," she said.

I finished my tea and headed towards my tent, smiling at how my mam always called Sheffield 'town', even though it was a city.

As I stowed my ball away safely in my tent that night, I was more pleased than I could ever remember about anything. Things were really looking up for me. School was bearable because of football and I even had a couple of friends, Samuel and now Joe since we'd patched things up between us. Even the hours in the classroom weren't a complete waste of time because I was learning to read and write. I knew I needed to do both of those things if I was going to be a footballer. There'd be important things I'd need to read, like rules and contracts, and Henry told me some of the famous players got asked to sign their names on football programmes and even cigarette packets. I'd already started to practise signing my name.

I was still trying get used to my amazing stroke of good fortune: not just to get a football in the first place, but to get a brand new one from my dad's friend and my dad not being able to complain about it was beyond a dream.

After I'd put my football away, I remembered the envelope that had been in the bag with it. I turned the paraffin lamp up, took the envelope out and opened it. Inside it was full of newspaper clippings. I recognized the name of the person all the articles were about straight away. It was Rab Howell! These were stories from the newspapers about his games. I noticed the dates were all from years ago.

I couldn't wait for the following day, to thank Uncle Jack for the ball and to talk to him about Rab Howell.

Even with the extra work, perhaps Henry courting and maybe even getting married soon would work in my favour. It might mean that my dad would see him more as an equal. I didn't mind that Henry was the golden son if it meant I could get away with playing football. Or maybe even that I could go and see a real football game at Sheffield United or the Wednesday, Maybe if I practised my writing, I could write a letter to Mr Howell and ask him what I should do. Maybe he'd even give me a job at his football club!

When Henry came into the tent, I was still awake: the excitement still hadn't worn off and I was keen to tell him how good my new football was. I also showed him the newspaper stories and told him about my plan to get Uncle Jack to help me send a letter to Mr Howell.

"Should I call him Mr Howell or Uncle, do you think?" I said with thoughts of a real footballer reading my letter and sending me one back racing through my head.

Henry's reply brought me back down to earth. "Look, Lijah," he said. "You need to get that daftness out of yer head. Me dad is not gonna let you be a footballer, so just enjoy it while yer can."

"But when you're married, he's not gonna bother about me, is he?" I retorted.

"Lijah, everything is changing so fast. No one knows what's gonna happen. We might all have to have jobs an' houses before too long."

"But Henry—"

"Lijah, don't let me mam or dad see them newspaper stories and pictures," Henry interrupted. "They'll go mad with yer. Hide 'em away and take them back to Mr Davis."

I realized there was no point arguing with Henry. There was clearly something on his mind which I didn't understand and I doubted he'd tell me even if I asked. I turned my thoughts back to football and fell asleep writing the letter in my head.

The next day I left school at dinner time, pretending I had a bad stomach as my dad had instructed. When I got to our camp, he already had the horse and cart ready. I hopped on to it and we set off towards Sheffield, me eating the sandwich my mam had given me. We were silent as my dad expertly drove us through a couple of busy places.

After a while he spoke. "You're taken with that ball, aren't yer?"

I just nodded in reply.

"I'm happy for yer, but don't forget that ball is just a *chavvies'* game. Yer getting older so yer have to be thinkin' like our Henry now."

"Aye," I said. What I really wanted to say was that it wasn't just a game, it was a sport. A proper sport. But I didn't because I didn't want to disrespect my father.

My dad picked up on my mood and tried to cheer me up with a couple of jokes, which didn't work as well as they usually did. He changed tack and asked me to start looking out for Uncle Jack's house. My dad knew the name of the road, but he couldn't recognize numbers. "Look out for number sixty-three … something villa."

We drove on to a wide street, more like an avenue with trees down the sides. The houses were joined together – terraced, I think they were called – but these weren't like the colliers' houses we usually called at. These were big and high with windows on the roof. The large windows at the bottom curved outwards, one on either side of the big front doors.

The house we were looking for was on the end of the row. I could see the number and the name *Athens Villa*. My reading was getting better, and I remembered that name, Athens, from a school lesson. It was a city in a country called Greece, where the people were clever at mathematics.

My dad pulled the horse and cart up outside and walked up the steps. He knocked loudly on the door, which was opened by a small thin woman who looked like she had the weight of the world on her shoulders. I guessed it must have been Uncle Jack's wife.

"He's not in," she said by way of greeting. "He's left it around the back for you. The gate's unlocked."

"Thank you, madam," my dad said, raising his hat to her as she slowly closed the front door.

We went around to the back of the house. My dad opened the heavy metal gate as I drove the cart through the opening, which led into a large cobbled yard with brick-built stables, one either side of an arched opening, where my dad told me the cart would be kept. We looked in and saw a ladder leading up to a hay loft.

"This place is better than some *Gorja*'s houses," he said in wonder.

I don't know what made me respond by saying, "Henry says everyone, including Travellers, might be living in houses soon."

My dad's face looked like thunder. "No such thing is gonna happen to us, I'll make sure of that. Henry and yer Uncle Billy dunno what they're talking about half the time with the daft ideas they get from *Gorjas*."

My dad located the metal and motioned for me to start picking it up and putting it on the back of the cart. Once it was loaded and roped on, we set off back

97

to the camp to sort through it properly. The journey was a slow and quiet one, as neither of us said a word.

Thirteen

The next morning, I finished my chores and had a bit of an early dinner. I thought I'd go thank Uncle Jack in person, as I hadn't got the chance to do it the day before.

"Tek that new mare; she's nearly right now," my dad said.

I put the bridle and saddle on her and set off. Hettie was a lovely animal: a good horse for riding and driving. If you wanted to get top money for them, they had to be good in any place, town or countryside, and able to understand what the owner wanted. We were going to have to sell her with Henry's wedding coming up.

I pulled her up outside of Uncle Jack's house and tied her to the metal railings. I walked up the front steps and knocked on the door. I waited a couple of minutes for someone to answer it.

"Young Lijah," Uncle Jack said, surprised. "Welcome, lad, come in."

He opened the door wider for me to enter. I hadn't been in many houses, but this one was definitely the biggest. It had a proper passageway, with a number of doors to other rooms. I followed him to a room that had a roaring fire and a large table.

"Betty!" he shouted. "We have a visitor."

The woman who answered the door yesterday came into the room followed by a young woman about the same age as Genty, dressed in what Henry called a parlour maid uniform. Uncle Jack's wife said, "Bring tea and cakes, Margaret."

"Yes ma'am," the young woman said as she scurried away. She soon returned bringing a plate of cakes which she placed on the table. "Tea's on its way, ma'am," she said as she turned and went back out of the room.

We'd seen servants come to the doors of big houses when we were collecting rag-and-bone, but I had never been served like this in my life.

We sat down on chairs at the table, waiting for the tea.

"This is young Lijah, Abe's lad."

"Are you the one who came yesterday?" Uncle Jack's wife said.

"Yes, madam," I said, copying the way my father spoke to *Gorja* women.

"I like that, good manners are important. So, to what do we owe the pleasure of your company?" Uncle Jack asked.

Although I didn't really know what he'd said, I guessed that he was asking why I'd come. "The ball is *kushti* … er … I mean, very good. Thank you, Uncle Jack."

I noticed Uncle Jack's wife's eyebrows raise in surprise when I called her husband Uncle Jack. He noticed it too. "The Uncle thing is a sign of respect in their world," he said.

Margaret came and placed a large tea pot and tiny cups down on the table.

"Thank you," Uncle Jack said to her, before turning back to me. "C'mon, don't be shy! These cakes are for eating and the tea for drinking," he said as he poured me a cup of tea. "So, you like the football, eh?"

"Oh, I love it, Uncle." I went on to tell him about playing with it on the common.

"I also brought this back for you," I said as I laid the envelope on the table.

"Those clippings are yours to keep if you want them," he said.

"I do but…" I hesitated not knowing exactly how to say it. "I'm not sure me mam or dad would want me to have them."

"Ah, well, tell you what I'll do. I'll keep them here for you and you can come and look at them anytime you want. I'll even read them out for you and tell you why your mam and dad maybe aren't big fans of Rab Howell."

"Thank you, Uncle Jack. That would be good," I said.

He smiled and then his expression turned serious. "So, you like your football and you can play a bit, according to your brother. Don't take this the wrong way, lad, but there's plenty of lads in this town who can play a bit, but only a few who can play well, and without seeing you play, I don't know which one you are and if you're serious about being a footballer."

I didn't know exactly what to say to that apart from, "Football is the only thing I want to do. I think my heart will break if I can't do it."

"We must get you a game then, lad," he said smiling.

I finished my tea and cake and followed Uncle Jack around to the back of his house. He showed me the spare stable to put the mare in, then we set off on foot to catch a tram towards Brightside.

As the tram rattled along towards our destination, we talked non-stop about football. He was asking me a whole load of questions about my favourite teams; did

I know this player and that player; did I understand the offside rule. I answered every question easily.

"I'm puzzled why you haven't tried out for your local team."

I thought for a second about making up an answer but decided to tell the truth. "Thing is, Uncle, see we … because of who we are, we don't really mix and my dad…"

My voice trailed away. I couldn't really put it into words without feeling disloyal.

Uncle Jack nodded. "I understand it might be difficult for a Gypsy lad, but I'm sure I can help with that," he said.

It was good that he understood how hard it might be for a Traveller person like me. Whether he also understood that I felt it was too close to home with regards to my father, or that if I failed to get in the team my dreams would be shattered and I'd be reminded of it every day we lived there, I wasn't so sure.

When we got off the tram and started walking, Uncle Jack spoke again. "Good to see you've got your strong boots on."

I didn't realize the importance of that until we turned the corner, then went down a tight little ginnel between two shops that opened up on to a playing field.

A football game was in progress. I did a quick count and saw the two teams had the right number of players and someone was even acting as the referee.

We stood watching the game. There were some good players. Both keepers were forced to make a few good saves. I could feel my muscles twitch as I watched the players head up the field into the opponents' half and then take shots on goal.

Uncle Jack and I talked all the way through the game, discussing individual players and the teams: Wincobank Wanderers and Brightside Valiants. At half-time, a few people sauntered over to talk to the players on each side while they had a rest and a drink, or a smoke of a cigarette or pipe.

One of the older men came over to talk to us. He and Uncle Jack obviously knew each other well.

"Jack," the man said, putting his hand out. After they shook, he reached his hand towards mine. "Who's this?" he asked as we shook hands.

"Harry, this is Lijah. He's a player – can you give him ten minutes in the second half?"

"Want to see what he's made of, eh?"

Uncle Jack nodded. I got the feeling that I wasn't the first player to have been tried out here.

"What position do yer play, young man?"

"Anywhere sir ... but I like to score goals if I can."

Harry laughed. "I'll put yer up front, see if you can get us a winner."

As Harry walked back towards his team, Uncle Jack said, "This is yer chance, lad. Now be careful; these are tough lads — colliers and steel workers. They're not keen on outsiders and yer not as big as them."

I nodded and just waited for my chance.

Harry waved me over to where the other lads were huddled around him, waiting to start the second half.

"This is Lijah. I'm givin' him a try playin' up front. Ernie, you can sit out for ten minutes."

"Looks like a foreigner," the lad called Ernie said, looking me up and down. He walked away without saying another word.

"He's a little 'un, Harry," said one of the team, who wasn't much bigger than me.

I didn't know where I'd heard it before, but a saying came to mind.

"It's not the size of the dog in the fight, it's the size of the fight in the dog," I said.

They all laughed, including Harry. I knew Uncle Jack was watching me and I was starting to pick up from other people how important he was. People listened to him — he had money, and that went a long way in terms of respect in a city like Sheffield.

The other team kicked off and I was on that ball like a greyhound out of the traps. I took it off one of them within the first minute and ran like my life depended on it. In a way it did – the life I wanted, anyway. I dodged a couple of tackles and a body charge that would have probably put me in hospital if I hadn't switched direction. Now it was me and the keeper.

Remembering to keep on side, I let one of the other players catch me up. He darted around me, trying to defend the goal. He and the keeper had no chance.

I knew that ball was going to cross the line as soon as it hit my foot.

Goal!

Harry kept me on until the end of the game, even though I was a marked man. The other team were trying to close me down at every opportunity and I spent my time passing the ball as soon as I had it.

"Well done, lads," said Uncle Jack at the end of the match. "A good game was that. I'll give Harry here enough money to stand you all a sandwich and drink at the cafe."

There was a round of 'thank yous' from the lads as they walked off, leaving me, Uncle Jack and Harry.

"You fancy coming next week, Lijah? I can give you a full game," Harry asked.

Before I could answer, Uncle Jack butted in. "No offence, Harry, but you saw how he played today. He's got his sights set higher than this."

Harry looked disappointed. "He could learn a lot here from the Valiants."

"With the right training, this lad is going to the top. He's the next Rab Howell, cut from the same cloth," Uncle Jack declared. Then, after thinking about it for a moment, he seemed to change his mind. "It couldn't hurt to play a few more games with this lot. What say you, Lijah?"

"Yes, please," I said.

"Champion," said Harry, shaking my hand.

On the way back to Uncle Jack's home, we talked about every aspect of the game I'd just played in. He was impressed by what he'd seen, but also told me that there was a lot of work to be done if I was going to be a professional.

As I led Hettie the mare from the stable back on to the street, Uncle Jack clapped me on the back. "We'll talk again soon, Lijah, make a plan, eh?"

"Yes, Uncle," I said as I turned the mare towards our camp. I rode home with my spirits so high it felt like I was on a flying horse.

That night as I lay in bed basking in the good feelings of the day, I was thinking about what Uncle

Jack had told me about Rab Howell, the man who was becoming my hero. He was born in a wagon in a little village called Dore to a family like mine; he grew up in a similar way; he went to school and didn't like it any more than I did; his dad didn't want him there. Somehow he got into playing football. Uncle Jack said he was a pioneer, which meant somebody who does something first. There was a lot more and I was all ears.

Nobody knows how he became so good at football, but he was, and he played for a proper team called Rotherham Swifts and Sheffield United and even England and he scored a goal for them. "Are you sure he was a Romani like me?" I asked Uncle Jack at least three times, especially as he told me Rab Howell had lived in a house in Sheffield and not a wagon or a tent. He proved it by reading it from one of the newspaper clippings and showed me the word so I could learn it.

I had so many questions racing around my brain; why, when this man had lived the life I wanted, was no one in family talking about him? Why, if he was so famous and earning a good living from it, was my dad so against me playing it? Why had it taken a *Gorja* person to tell me?

Those questions were soon answered, when we got onto what Uncle Jack called the second half of Rab's time in football. He had played three very important games, things had gone wrong and he'd been accused of letting the other teams win on purpose. Some people said he'd been paid to lose and was a cheat. Uncle Jack said, "But he certainly wasn't. It was most likely to do with what was going on at the club. Rab never really fit in; he didn't see the owners as his betters and spoke out, asked for more money and was seen as a troublemaker."

Then Uncle Jack lowered his voice and hesitated before he carried on: "I don't even know whether I should be telling you this, Lijah, but I reckon the way your reading is coming on, you'll be able to read it for yourself soon ... I don't expect you to fully understand it, but adults sometimes aren't always the most... He was married with children and ... well, he started a new relationship with another woman and he signed for Liverpool and moved away from Sheffield."

I was shocked but it finally made sense why I'd never heard of Rab before and my mam and especially my dad didn't want me to play the game.

Fourteen

Everything started to happen very fast after that. Henry announced to us all that he and Genty were engaged. My mam and dad were thrilled about it, not only because Genty's family was what they called 'Kushti Folki', but because Genty herself, with her earning power, would ensure that she and Henry would be able to keep themselves and any children they had very well. I had mixed feelings about it. I would lose Henry as my best friend and I'd have to do more work, but I was happy for him. And besides, I had Uncle Jack to talk to now about my true love, football.

Uncle Jack continued to help me with my reading and writing and educating me about football and also helping me to understand what happened to my hero Rab Howell.

I had to pinch myself every time I thought about my good fortune. In a matter of weeks, I'd gone from being someone who just played football at school to someone who'd had four games with proper good players. I'd scored in every one of them for the Brightside Valiants and even been called their star player.

After my last game, where I scored the winning goal, Uncle Jack had even said, "You've still a way to go and we might have to lie about your age, but you could be playing for money by the end of next year."

That was all the encouragement I needed. I didn't care what my mam or dad thought about Rab Howell. He was my hero and I was going to be a professional like him and maybe even play for my country.

"Uncle Jack, can I take those newspaper cuttings back?" I asked one afternoon, when we'd gone back to Uncle Jack's house after a game.

"Course you can, lad," he said smiling. He went to get the envelope for me.

"Here's something else to put with them," he said as he handed me a folded piece of writing paper. "All the dates of the games and the one I've underlined in red is the most important game of your life so far. There'll be people from football clubs, proper clubs, watching you. If all goes well, who knows what might happen next."

I stared wide eyed listening to him. This was it: my big chance.

"If you think I'm ready, Uncle Jack, I'll not let you down."

"Aye I do, and you'd better not. I've put my reputation and money on the line for this – chance of a lifetime."

I put the envelope and list of dates safely in my coat pocket and set off back home.

Even though we knew Henry's fiancée Genty and her family very well, the engagement still had to be made official, which is why her parents, Dennis and Jemima, came over to our camp one Sunday afternoon to have a bite to eat and discuss where and when the wedding was going to take place.

The three of them came on a flat cart pulled by a very nice cob, which I guessed was their best horse. My mam had once again got out the best china, along with the little table and a tablecloth. All of the children and young people in our family had been told to be on our best behaviour. We had to say hello to Dennis and Jemima and Genty, then go about our chores and leave them be.

I looked on from a distance as they all sat around the table having tea. I could see how nervous Henry was – he wasn't eating anything. Genty's father was known as a man who liked a drink and it wasn't long before he, my father and Henry walked off in the direction of the ale house, no doubt to discuss the financial side of things. I knew they'd talk about how Henry was going to be able to look after Genty – whether he had enough money to provide suitable accommodation. They'd also discuss whether Henry was going to join their family's camp or whether Genty would join ours. I hoped she'd come and live with us – I'd miss Henry if he went away.

My mam, Genty and Genty's mother moved into the wagon to continue their conversations along similar lines. I took this as an opportunity to go off and practise with my football. Hopefully everyone would soon be so busy getting ready for the wedding that no one would miss me when I was at the match with Uncle Jack.

The next day, Henry told me that everything had been agreed. He and Genty were definitely getting married. They had decided that she would join us until she was expecting a child, then they would go and travel or camp with her family. Henry also let slip that her mam and dad were getting fed up with the travelling life and it wouldn't take much for them to become settled.

"You wouldn't become settled though, would you, Henry?" I asked.

"Nah, goin' to Hull tomorrow to order and put a deposit on a new tent."

I congratulated him and told him how pleased I was that he and his wife would be living with us. I didn't tell him it was a huge relief, and how I hoped it would help me with my plans to become a professional footballer.

My dad came over with a big smile on his face. "Yer goin' to have to work hard now, son, with a wife to keep and some *chavvies* before too long, eh?" Henry smiled and nodded in return.

"Better get that mare ready for sale, Lijah," my dad said.

"Aye, Dad, she's nearly ready," I replied.

Travelling people didn't have long engagements; they got married as soon as everything had been agreed between them and their families.

It was clear Genty was a very good organizer and through my mam's connections with the local church, she'd even persuaded the parson to marry them. None of this, or any of the other arrangements about the wedding, was of much interest to me, until my mam told me the date.

It was the same afternoon as the most important game of my life. Uncle Jack had told me important people would be watching and he and Harry had put up some money to give to the goal scorers.

I checked the date with Henry in case my mam had got it wrong. I even asked my Uncle Billy, hoping beyond hope that Henry had got it wrong, too. They all said the same day. Now I was stuck.

"What yer so interested about the date for? Yer getting married yerself on the quiet?" my Uncle Billy said laughing. I laughed along at his joke, but inside I was in turmoil.

I had to play in that game, but I had to be at Henry's wedding. I tried to work it all ways in my mind, how I could do both, but as my dad often used to joke, you can't ride two horses with one backside. The closer the date of the wedding got, the more pressure I felt.

And then I had the most amazing stroke of luck. The parson said he couldn't marry them in the afternoon – he would have to do it in the morning instead. He didn't say why he had to change the time, but I didn't care because it meant that I could go to the wedding at the church, go back to the camp to get one of the horses and get to Uncle Jack's in time to play the match.

Uncle Jack knew about the wedding and had already given Henry some money as a present. Even though he wasn't going to be at the wedding itself, he would come to the camp afterwards for the food, music and dancing.

We had many conversations about all kinds of things on our travels to and from the football games.

"I had a son who died from a seizure when he was eight years old," he told me one day.

I told him how sorry I was about his son and asked him what he was like. My mam and dad both said that when tragedies happen you should talk about them; it makes sure the person who died isn't forgotten.

"He was hooked on football, Lijah."

"I think me and him would have got along very well, Uncle Jack," I said. Even though talking about his son had made him sad, he smiled and said, "I'm sure you would ... I'm sure you would. It makes me feel better when I see you play."

And play I did, at every opportunity. Uncle Jack had bought me proper football boots and a jersey and some trousers they called football knickers. To be fair to him, he left the decision about playing the big game on the day of the wedding to me, but I could tell he wanted me to choose the game by the way he said it. "Now I won't blame you if you choose not to leave your brother's wedding. But sometimes, Lijah, we have to make sacrifices to get where we need to go. I'll leave it up to you."

I lost sleep over it. I couldn't talk to anyone about it, not even Henry. I tried to pretend that the wedding was a little thing, and no one would mind if I wasn't there, but I knew I was lying to myself.

All the way up to the day of the wedding, my thoughts were going backwards and forwards. Sometimes I thought I could go through with my plan and other times I knew I couldn't. I was so torn between doing the right thing with my family and following my heart. How could I choose between football and family?

I couldn't bring myself to tell Uncle Jack what was happening inside my head, so he just went on talking about the game and planning what would happen after. He thought I might even get signed by a proper club.

The day of the wedding arrived, and I still didn't know what I was going to do. I felt like a trapped animal. I had visions of the rest of the team standing around, wondering where I was. They might even worry that I'd been run over on the way there, or even worse, that I wasn't really that interested in football. And when Uncle Jack told them I was at a wedding instead … some of them would understand, but some of them would see it as me not being committed enough. I'd never been to a wedding in a church before and I was already uncomfortable sitting in my best clothes watching Henry stood at the front looking more nervous than I'd ever seen him, waiting as we all were for Genty to join him and the parson so they could do the marriage. It all seemed to be taking a very long time. Then the organ music started, my dad nudged me to stand up and soon Genty joined my brother, looking like a princess. My mam and Genty's mam were both dabbing their eyes with handkerchiefs.

All I could think about was getting to the football game.

Soon the wedding was over and everyone went back to the camp. The women were making tea, the men were cooking over the fires and the children were playing with each other. Soon everyone was eating and drinking.

I looked around to check no one was watching me, then I swear that my feet started moving on their own, heading towards my tent where I kept my football kit in a bag. I slung the bag over my shoulder, quickly walked behind the wagons and led a horse away from the camp. As soon as I thought it was safe, I rode as fast as I could to Uncle Jack's.

His wife told me he'd already gone to the match and handed me some money that he'd left for me for the tram just in case I turned up. I put my horse in his stable and jumped on a tram heading towards the game. I willed the tram to hurry as it wove through the busy streets.

When I finally arrived, the match was just about to start. I had to get changed in double quick time. Harry and Uncle Jack were not pleased.

"Get on now – up front!" Harry said, physically shoving me on to the field.

I did as he asked and went straight for the ball, but the other player kept it turned and sent it back up the field. I chased it but couldn't catch it. I was out of breath already.

The ball came towards me. I trapped it, tackled an opposing player and went for a shot on goal – it went wide.

My teammates were as disappointed as I was, but we pressed on. Still, for some reason I couldn't turn myself onto full power. I'd missed a couple of good passes and let their forward turn me, which resulted in him scoring. They were two-nil up at half-time.

Harry was not at all pleased with any of us. "I don't know what you think you're doing out there, but it isn't football. Yer playing like a bunch of little children! Buck yer ideas up or we're gonna lose this game. And you, Lijah, whatever's the matter with you, get it sorted and quick."

I looked over to where Uncle Jack was talking with a couple of men; they all looked at me. I felt bad that I was letting everyone down and that pressure didn't do anything to help me in the second half. My playing got even worse. I missed two more opportunities to score and then, even worse, in the last few minutes of the game I scored an own goal when trying to clear a shot that the goalkeeper had told me to leave for him. And that was pretty much the end of the game that had been a disaster from start to finish.

When Harry gathered us all together, all I could say was sorry to my team and to both him and Uncle Jack. What I couldn't tell them was that I had been so worried about my family finding out I'd left the celebrations, I couldn't focus on the game at all because I was overwhelmed with guilt. I got my horse from Uncle Jack's and rode home as quickly as I could. I didn't even stop to change out of my football kit.

It was as I was trying to sneak back into camp that my dad spotted me.

"Tie that horse up and come over here," he said in a calm and controlled voice which he used when he was furious.

I did as he asked. It was only as I walked over to

him that I saw he had my football. He picked it up and held it in front of him.

"See this? I told yer it was nothing but trouble and look what it's caused. You've been off playing football instead of being with yer family." My dad's voice was getting louder now and he wasn't bothering to disguise his anger. Everyone was looking at us. "Is this worth more than yer family, is it? Well, is it?"

I shook my head.

"Right, I want you to watch and listen. You are not playing this game any more. You are not going to school any more. You're going to grow up and be a proper Traveller man."

And to emphasize his point, he took his wood carving knife out of his pocket and plunged its sharp blade into my football. Then, still glaring at me, he threw it on the fire, where it immediately started to smoke.

I wanted to run and grab it, but I knew I couldn't. I walked slowly past everyone, not daring to catch anyone's eye, and went and sat in my tent. I felt so ashamed and angry with myself. How could I possibly put all of this right?

Fifteen

My dad was serious about taking me out of school and my mam, despite her earlier concerns, agreed with him. I didn't know what was happening with Uncle Jack. My dad told me not to go to his house and he hadn't been up to the camp either, even though I'd told my family it was my choice to go to that game and not Uncle Jack's fault.

No one mentioned football. It was as if it had never existed, but I missed it more than I could have imagined. I thought about it all the time. I even dreamed about it when I slept.

Even Henry was acting differently towards me. We didn't laugh and joke the way we used to. It seemed like we were just people who went out to work together rather than the friends we used to be. At first, I thought it was because I had caused trouble at his wedding, but there seemed to be more to it than that. Henry wasn't one to hold a grudge and I was sure he was keeping a secret.

Genty had moved to our camp. She was making more clothes and had even sold one of her 'garments', as she called them, to a shop in the city. They'd said if it sold, they would order two more from her. Even though Henry was the best caller for rag-and-bone I'd ever known, it was as if he'd lost the desire to do it. He kept asking me to go out with him and we'd split what we earned. My dad was pleased with this arrangement. He saw it as Henry teaching me to be a man and keeping me away from football.

Talking to Henry every day on the cart, I got the feeling that, as he and Genty were falling more in love with each other, they were falling out of love with the Travelling way of life. It wasn't anything specific, just little things like complaining about having to carry water, dealing with the mud and the cold and the damp, and the ever-present risk of being moved on: things we'd been used to since we were children. Things I thought we just took in our stride. He kept talking about having regular money every week and somewhere for Genty to sell her clothes. I was starting to get that feeling again that he was keeping a secret. Worse still, I thought I knew what it was.

Sitting down for tea one night, when usually I'd have been so hungry I'd have cleared my plate in a few minutes flat, the food no longer tasted the same. I just felt cut off from the other life I'd had. No more school, no more going to see Uncle Jack and no more football of any description. I'd lost a huge part of my life.

As I handed my half-eaten food back to my mam, I knew she knew what was wrong with me, but she couldn't, or wouldn't, do anything about it.

"You'll find something better than football, son," she said. "Something that'll make your head and your heart sing just as much. Look at Henry with Genty – two proper love birds they are."

My mam meant well, but I knew I'd never find anything as good as football.

And so the weeks went on. Henry and Genty spent more time with each other. When they weren't in Sheffield selling the clothes she made, they were out looking for material to make more.

One evening, as I was just about to attend to my chores, I saw Uncle Jack pull on to the camp with his horse and trap. He fastened the reins and walked over to the fire.

"Hey up, young Lijah," he said smiling. He reached out his hands to the flames to warm them.

"Hello, Uncle Jack," I said. Out of the corner

of my eye, I saw my dad striding towards us. I wanted to run because I knew there was going to be trouble.

"Evening, Abe," Uncle Jack said.

My dad just nodded.

"Sorry I didn't get to the wedding reception," Uncle Jack said. "I had a lot of things on – been very busy. I've just come to see why young Lijah hasn't been coming to football."

"I'll tell you why, Jack," my dad said angrily, his arms folded across his chest. "Because he picked a daft *Gorja* game of football over his family. And do you know what I did when I found out?"

The smile had disappeared from Uncle Jack's face as my dad carried on. "I burst that ball you gave him and I threw it on the fire. So now you know."

Uncle Jack took a step back. There was a look of confusion and fear on his face.

"I thought the wedding had finished, I didn't think Lijah was going to be late … if I'd have known I'd have brought him back myself Abe," he said quietly.

My dad took a deep breath. "Makes no difference," he said in a slightly calmer voice. "The damage is done. He's not playing football any more. He's a Traveller boy and that's the end of it."

But Uncle Jack didn't seem ready to give up. "Abe,

the lad could be a professional. He could earn his living. Maybe even get rich."

"What? And end up like Rab Howell?" my dad said, leaving that hanging in the air.

That was the first time I'd heard my dad mention my football hero's name. I wanted to jump up and tell my dad that Rab Howell was a genius. That he had been made out to be bad when he wasn't! But I couldn't say a word. I knew it would only make things worse.

"Well, if that's the way you feel, then there's nowt I can do," said Uncle Jack.

"It is," said my dad. He took another deep breath. "And I don't want you coming here any more, Jack, or Lijah going anywhere near you or football."

Uncle Jack looked at me and I quickly looked down. By the time I lifted my head, he was already walking away. He got into his trap and set off.

As I watched him leave, I saw my hopes and dreams leave with him.

I'm sure my dad thought his troubles were over once he'd got me away from football, but they were only starting. Only this time it wasn't me causing the trouble. A few days after Uncle Jack's visit, as I returned from doing an errand for my mam, I heard my dad and Henry shouting at each other. My mam and Genty were trying to calm them down.

They fell silent as I approached.

"What's going on?" I asked. Henry and my dad were both red in the face.

"Go on, Henry. Tell 'im what yer doing."

But I already knew because Henry had told me the night before.

"I've got some news for you, Lijah," Henry had said as we checked on the horses. "Me and Genty ... well ... there's only one way to say it."

"She's expecting? You're havin' a *chavvie*," I'd said.

"No, no ... we're settlin'. We're gettin' a house with Genty's mam and dad."

I'd been shocked but, somehow, not surprised. In a way, I'd been expecting it. I was stuck for words at first, trying to take it in. There was a silence between us for a moment.

"I can't do it any more, Lijah," said Henry. He'd put his head in his hands. "We've got to make the move now. Genty wants a shop for her clothes. You can't sell them on the road. And I need regular wages."

"When are you leaving?" I'd asked.

"A week."

"So you won't be travelling with us for summer," I said.

128

He shook his head.

"Have you told Mam and Dad?"

He shook his head again and looked like he was going to cry.

I put my hand on his shoulder. "It'll be all right," I said, even though I knew it wouldn't be. My dad was not going to be happy.

Sure enough, the conversation looked to be going very badly.

As my dad continued to yell, "Go on tell yer brother," Henry had to go through the charade of telling me.

I could see Genty following the argument closely but hanging back from saying anything. Maybe she was seeing if her husband really wanted the move to a settled life as much as she did.

"I'm settling down with Genty and her mam and dad and we're not travelling any more."

"Oh," I said, unsure how to react.

My mam stood silently as my dad threw his hands up in the air in exasperation.

"I don't care any more what yer do," he said, looking from Henry's face to mine. "You, with yer house and job and you, with yer football. A couple of proper little *Gorjas*, that's all you are."

And with that he walked away.

My mam looked at us, tears glistening in her eyes. "He doesn't mean that," she said. "He's just angry; give him a bit of time to let him calm down."

The next morning there was a bad atmosphere around the camp. My mam and dad were unusually quiet, as was everyone else, though nobody mentioned the conversation from the night before. By dinner time, neither Henry nor Genty had come out of their tent. There was no thought of going out to work – everyone knew that when there was an issue on the camp, it was considered bad luck to go out. Even if you did, your mind wouldn't be on it anyway.

We all busied ourselves with our chores, but the atmosphere remained terrible. It was made worse because it was less than a week before we were going to set off on our spring and summer travels.

A week went by, and Henry and my dad didn't pass a word between them. We packed up everything, just like always, and it was soon time to set off. It was such a wrench saying goodbye to Henry and Genty, knowing I wouldn't see them for months and that, when I did, they would be living in a house somewhere in Sheffield.

As we left them behind, my mam was crying, and I wanted to cry too.

The summer travelling, instead of being the usual

fun holiday, was a miserable affair. I missed Henry terribly and so did my dad even though he wouldn't admit it. My mam and dad found it very difficult telling our extended family about Henry and Genty. There was still some horse fairs and storytelling and music around the fire, but it just wasn't the same. I was counting the days to getting back to Sheffield – even though my dad had forbidden me from playing the game I loved, he couldn't stop me from watching it.

The thought of never playing football again would descend on me like a rain cloud and then I'd be busy making and selling things, doing my usual work as well as Henry's; making sure all the animals were taken care of and forgetting about it for a while until it came back again. I still had my envelope of newspaper clippings and read them religiously. I believed I must know more about the man than any of his fans. I learned about his move to Liverpool and then to Preston where disaster struck when he broke his leg. He'd had to give up the game he loved and start a business instead. Many times I thought about how Rab must have felt when he couldn't play any more but I knew he was a Romani like me, and we never give up.

Sixteen

The weather was turning. During the last few weeks of our travels the weather seemed determined to match our moods as the rain continued to come down day after day.

The first leaves were starting to fall from the trees and it was time to head back to Sheffield. I never thought the day would come when I was looking forward to going back to the city, but I was. I'd missed Henry and I'd missed football, even though I hadn't played a game since the last disastrous one. I had made a point of keeping myself fit and keeping up with all the teams by reading newspapers that other people had finished with. I still had the envelope full of news stories about Rab Howell, which I knew almost by heart now I'd read them so many times.

I was secretly hoping that my dad would relent and let me play football again.

There was one thing I wouldn't have to bother

with when I got back, and that was school. I was past the age now. I had started earning my own money and was included in the men's talk the same way Henry had been.

"We're not going back to Ecclesfield," my dad said, when we were a day away from our usual stopping place. He'd had word that other Travellers had beaten us to it. "We'll head to Wincobank. I've got someone who's saved us some pitches."

More Travelling people were coming to Sheffield, so the stopping places were becoming crowded. Maybe Henry was right that we'd all end up in houses anyway.

As soon as we got set up properly on our new camp, me and my mam went over to see Henry and Genty. My dad decided not to go.

I heard him say to my mam, "How can I go an' see my lad in a house? Be like seeing a man in prison."

I wondered if my dad felt that he'd failed Henry, rather than Henry failing him.

"C'mon, we'll be getting there tomorrow if you don't hurry up with that cart," my mam said, bringing me back from my thoughts.

I harnessed the horse and attached the cart and we set off to Henry's. My mam had the number and the name of the road.

134

"I'm glad I wrapped up," my mam said, pulling her big wool coat around herself and retying her headscarf as we picked up speed towards our destination. I was having to concentrate on driving. I'd forgotten how busy the city was and we were going around the edge of it. It was cold for the first week of October and I was glad of my big coat.

We passed a number of factories and wondered which one Henry was working in and how he was dealing with it. I had a hundred questions for him about what it was like living like a *Gorja* among them.

"What's wrong?" my mam said as I pulled the horse up. I couldn't tell her that it was because I'd just noticed we were in front of Uncle Jack's house. I hadn't realized we were in this area, and it had given me quite a start, reminding me of my last game of football and all that had passed after.

"Nothing," I said as I tapped the reins on the horse's rump. We lurched forward towards Henry's house, which we soon found on a street that was much narrower and less grand than Uncle Jack's avenue.

Genty and Henry welcomed us into their house. I couldn't get over the fact that my brother lived here. He had an upstairs and a bedroom, gas lights, a water pump in the kitchen and a toilet outside in the backyard. Apart from chopping a few sticks for the fire, there were no other jobs to do. The women had their catch up in the front room, and we stayed in the back room.

"It's so good to see you, brother," he said.

"You mean *phrala*, not brother," I said reminding him of our Romani language.

"Aye, I've not forgotten it that quick. Me and Genty still speak it in the house," he said.

"I'm only joshing yer," I said.

"I know," he replied, although I'm not sure he did.

"What's it like having a job in a factory?" I said.

"I dunno," he replied smiling. "I work down the pit."

"A collier!" I blurted out.

I couldn't imagine being born and brought up like us and ending up down a coal mine. I didn't say that to Henry, but he must have read the thoughts from my face.

"Beggars can't be choosers," he said.

I thought of reminding him that we weren't beggars, we were proud Traveller people, but thought better of it.

"It's good money, Lijah, an' regular. We need to

pay for the rent here every week. Besides, it's not for ever as me an' Genty are both earning, and it won't be long before we can get the shop she wants. Then we can live over the top of it. You could come an' live with us if you like."

I tried to imagine what it would be like living with Henry again.

"How's me dad?" he asked, changing the subject.

"He's all right. I think he'd be happy if you came back," I said.

Henry shook his head. "As hard as it is at the moment working down the pit, I would never go back to travelling. Being among *Gorjas* and working with Genty, I've started to see things in a different way. The world is changing. There are more choices, even for people like us."

"Well, it was my choice to play football and look where that got me," I said.

"Lijah, just so you know, I don't hold any grudge about the wedding. I'm glad you went to the game. In fact, I've got some news for you." He grinned at me. "I've been talking to Jack Davis. He's been helping me and Genty learn about buying a shop. I told him you were coming today and he'd like to see you."

"I don't know ... what'd me dad think?" I replied.

"Lijah, you have to be your own man. Do what

you want to do. Our dad has always done that and so should you."

"I don't know Henry. I'm not sure I can," I said feeling very confused but also as if a little crack of light had opened up in a dark tunnel.

"Look, if you come with me round to Jack's now, I'll come up to the camp and speak to our dad. Deal?" He put his hand out for me to shake it.

I took his hand. "Deal," I said, wondering what I'd let myself in for.

Henry told Genty and my mam that we were going to see a neighbour. Ten minutes later, we were in Uncle Jack's house drinking tea and talking as if the trouble at the camp had never happened.

"Harry doesn't hold any grudges," said Uncle Jack. "After I told him about the wedding, he said to tell you that you're welcome back any time."

I didn't know what to say to that, so I just nodded. We both knew that the football season was now in full swing and I should be playing.

"Jack, tell him about your plan," Henry said.

"I just thought if your dad could see you play, he'd realize how good you are and how much you enjoy it," Uncle Jack said, his voice full of optimism.

"Tell him about the other thing," Henry said.

Uncle Jack had a huge smile on his face as he

retrieved two pieces of paper from an envelope on the table. "These are two tickets to next week's United game..."

"Tell him the other bit!" said Henry, unable to contain his excitement.

"How would you like to go to the match, then come and have tea here afterwards and meet a certain Mr Rab Howell?"

I was speechless for a good minute as his words sank in. "Rab Howell is coming here to see you?" I finally choked out.

"He's coming to Sheffield on business to talk to me about opening a shop, but he wants to meet you."

I knew Rab was retired after breaking his leg playing for Preston, but he was still my football hero.

I looked at Henry. He was grinning from ear to ear. I thought in that moment that he was the best brother in the world. We sat around drinking tea and talking about football and Rab Howell, all of his greatest moments at Sheffield United and when he played for England. Uncle Jack had some more newspaper stories and photographs and even some quotes that his teammates had written about him.

Then he placed a book on the table. "I bought this for you."

I picked it up and read the cover: *Association Football* by Ernest Needham.

"Go to the page with the bookmark."

I did as he asked, then read the text about Rab Howell out loud. *"Perhaps he owes some of his inexhaustible vitality to his lucky parentage. Certain it is that no man is more untiring … should the outside man indulge in dribbling he sticks to him like a leech."*

"You know what that means, Lijah?"

"That he was lucky to come from Romani people?"

"Exactly," Uncle Jack said, smiling.

"We're gonna have to get back home now, Jack," Henry said, rising from his chair and I did the same.

"So, am I going to see you here next Saturday to go to the United game and meet Rab afterwards?"

"Yes, Uncle," I said, and we all shook hands.

"Take the book with you," he said, handing it to me.

As we walked back to Henry's house with the book firmly wedged under my arm, I couldn't stop talking about Rab Howell and what Ernest Needham had said. I was still trying to get over the fact that someone had written something so good about Rab and about us.

"I know, Lijah, imagine that, eh? And imagine

when someone writes about *you* in the papers," Henry said.

Now all he and I had to do was fix things with our dad and I could be back playing again.

Seventeen

The first thing I did was buy a new football from the money I'd been saving up. I needed to see if I still loved playing and if I still had the skill, otherwise there wouldn't be any point risking more family upset.

It took me half an hour to ride from our new camp to the woods I knew so well. The closer I got, the more excited I was to try out my new football. But I was also aware of what was riding on all of this. Self-doubt began to creep in. What if I wasn't as good as I thought I was? How could I meet my hero Mr Howell without feeling, or worse, *looking*, like a fraud?

With the horse tied up safely and munching on some oats, I threw the ball on the floor and took aim at one of the trees. As soon as my boot connected with the ball, I knew it was a perfect strike. It felt so good to see it speeding towards the tree and then making a splendid superbly accurate hit before rebounding. I ran towards it and struck it again mid-air, then chased it and tackled my way through the trees, jumping over the roots and imagining the trees were my opponents and I was being chased by an opposing team.

I played with the football until I was completely exhausted and covered in sweat. I sat down with my back against a beech tree to take a rest. I looked up at the sky, now turning overcast, and I knew what I had to do. Whatever the cost, I had to speak to my dad and tell him I needed to pursue my dream.

As I approached the camp, I could see and smell the smoke from the fires. My mam, and all the other women from the different families, would be cooking tea. I knew whatever it was, I wouldn't be able to eat anything until I had spoken to my dad. I had already decided to leave the family and go and stay with Henry if he refused to change his mind.

I jumped down off the horse and led it away as my mam came round the back of the big wagon.

"Lijah, I'm glad you're back. I've been worried! No one knew where you were," my mam said.

"Sorry, Mam, I lost track of time," I replied.

"Take this and go and get a wash and change yer shirt," she said, handing me a towel. "We've got guests coming for tea."

I went to go and wash myself, hoping it wasn't some of my mam's religious friends – they were nice enough people, but I was too tired and highly strung

144

for prayers. I just wanted to get things sorted out with my dad.

I carried a bowl of water into my tent, washed and changed my shirt. Stepping out, I saw Henry and Genty getting out of Uncle Jack's pony trap. I wondered if I was dreaming for a minute before I rushed over to see them.

My mam gestured for me and Henry to sit down on alder wood stools, as she seated Genty into one of the wooden chairs. My dad joined us around the fire without saying a word. We all focused on the pans and the delicious smells that were coming out of them. My mam came back, stirred the food a few times and then, standing with her hands on her hips, spoke into the awkward silence. "It's lovely to see you, Henry and Genty. Isn't it, Abe?" She stared pointedly at my dad who kind of grumbled and mumbled, "Aye."

"Before we have our food, Henry's got something to say, haven't you, love?" my mam said.

"I have, Mam," he said, winking at me. "Look, Dad. I know you weren't happy about me and Genty leaving and going into a house but it's something we had to do. We're still Romani people. We still think like Travellers, we still feel like Travellers and one day we might go back to travelling. But, for now, we want to start a business doing something different."

I could see my mam and dad, like me, were following every word Henry said.

"That story you told us, Dad, about where we come from – them people coming into England and entertaining King Henry VIII? That's what Lijah wants to do with his football. He's a proper good player, I mean he's good enough to make a living from it. What would you rather – him going out on a cart in all weathers or earning twice as much for running around after a ball and being treated like a prize racehorse?"

My dad found his voice. "I know you bought a new ball, Lijah, and I know you were practising this afternoon." My dad was a very well-known man and very concerned about his reputation. He always told people that if they saw either me or Henry getting up to any mischief to let him know. Unfortunately, people were always reporting things to him whether we were getting into mischief or not.

It was now or never: I had to tell him. "Dad, I *have* to play football. If I can't do that living with you, then I'm gonna have to move away."

"No, Lijah," my mam said, covering her mouth with her hand.

My dad's reaction took me by surprise; it was as if he knew this was going to happen.

"I knew when you took up with that football it was gonna cause trouble for me and you. That Rab Howell you're always talking about – you know what happened to him, don't yer? And you still want to do it," my dad said shaking his head.

Henry spoke again. "You can take back up with Jack Davis. He says he's got some business to put your way for the winter – wants to meet with yer on Saturday."

"It couldn't hurt just to meet with the man," my mam said.

"He's been good to us – like a proper uncle," said Genty. "He lent us his trap to come here, and he's helping us set up our business."

It was clear my dad was weighing up the options and hadn't yet decided what to do; he was outnumbered, that was for certain.

Henry, the clever person he was, had saved the best until last. "And there's another reason why we should all be getting along and back to how we were. Me and Genty are expecting. You're going to be a granddad."

As if he couldn't help it, a huge smile spread across my dad's face. He, along with the rest of us, got up to hug Genty and Henry, congratulating them on their brilliant news. It'd been a while since I'd seen my mam and dad so happy. "Lord help us if the new *chavvie* turns out to be a footballer like our Lijah."

Everyone laughed.

And that was it. We were all back together again and, even though my dad hadn't said it in words, he'd given his blessing for me to start playing football again.

Before Henry left, we went off for a moment on our own. "Make sure you get our dad to Jack's for one o'clock on Saturday," he said. "And make sure you have those two tickets for the game."

"What about Uncle Jack?" I asked.

Henry smiled "Jack Davis is so well known in football he doesn't need a paper ticket for any game in this city; his name is his ticket."

Saturday came around quickly and me and my dad set off towards Uncle Jack's. As Henry had instructed, I had the two tickets stored safely in the inside pocket of my jacket, underneath my overcoat.

It was clear from the smell of the cold air that winter was on its way. I steered the horse into Uncle Jack's avenue and then up the side road towards the backyard.

"I'll open the gate," my dad said as he jumped off the cart.

Once in the yard, I started undoing the harness. "We won't be stopping that long," my dad said.

"I want to give him a proper rest. He ain't that

young any more," I replied, and my dad nodded.

Henry and Uncle Jack came out of the back door of the house together. They both shook hands with me and my dad.

"Come in out of the cold for a drink and something to eat," Uncle Jack said, leading us towards the door he'd come out of.

Once inside, I got the surprise of my life. There in the flesh was Rab Howell.

I couldn't speak. I just stared at him like he was a statue. I'd looked at his pictures so long many times that he didn't seem real. The actual Rab Howell, my hero. He wasn't as tall as me – he must have been about five foot five – but he seemed like a giant standing there in Uncle Jack's house. His short brown hair perfectly barbered, he was clean shaven and wearing an expensive suit. He was smiling at me, and I couldn't have been more surprised if one of the statues in the city had come alive. I'd only ever seen him pictured in his football clothes. I had a million thoughts racing through my head: was I dreaming? Was this really real? My heart was beating fast and my mouth had gone dry. I knew I was staring at him, but I couldn't help it.

Henry told me later that the original plan was for us to meet Rab after the game, but he had arrived on the earlier train, so they had come to Uncle Jack's house first.

"Rab Howell," Rab said, holding his hand out to my dad.

"Abe Vesh," my dad said, taking it with a frown. He glanced at Uncle Jack and for a moment I thought he might take a swing at him. I could tell he was even more shocked than me and trying to keep his anger in check. I knew my dad wouldn't want to be seen to be disrespectful to another Romani man even if he was a footballer he didn't like.

Rab sensed the atmosphere and tried to calm things down. "I've been hearin' all about this *chavo*. Jack here reckons you might even be better than me," he said followed by a huge laugh. My dad's mouth twitched, as if he might have wanted to smile, too.

"You got a fan there," said Uncle Jack. He poured a beer for my dad, Rab and himself.

After a slow start, Rab and my dad got on like a house on fire, speaking in a mixture of English, and Romanes, our language, talking about Sheffield and how Rab was going to start a business in the city. He also told us about all the rumours and all the things people had made up about him when he'd left Sheffield a few years before. While my dad, Uncle Jack and Henry were talking business I managed to overcome my shyness and have a conversation with Rab. "Do I call you Mr Howell or Uncle Rab?" I asked.

"Up to you," he replied.

"I'll call you Mr Howell like they did in the newspapers," I said.

I told him how Uncle Jack had given me the newspaper clippings and told me everything he knew about Rab's life and career. "I hope you didn't believe that rubbish about cheating," he said in a serious tone.

"No, Mr Howell, it didn't make sense to me that you'd do that."

As well as sharing lots of tips, giving me advice on how to improve my game and avoid getting into some of the trouble he had, he said, "Don't let anyone stop you from following your dreams. Despite the trouble I had, I wouldn't have missed being a professional footballer for the world. Sometimes you have to take a risk or you will never know what you could have accomplished."

I kept nodding along, taking it all in.

"And one more thing, Lijah. You could be the Romani player who makes the game popular among our people and no one else will have the troubles we've had. Jack told me about your troubles with your family. Do you want me to have a word with your dad for you?"

I shook my head – just listening to Rab had given me all the confidence I needed to do it myself. "Thank you, Mr Howell, but I need to do it for myself," I replied.

He smiled and shook my hand.

I interrupted the conversation my dad was having with Uncle Jack and Henry, "Dad, can I have a word?" I said as he followed me over to the door to where we came in.

I'd never felt so confident or grown up in my life. "Dad, I know you don't like football, but I know you love me, and I have to play football. I'll make you proud of me with it. I won't get into trouble; I know how to avoid that. I'll stay a Romani – it's not what work you do; it's what's in your heart. I want you to come to the football with us. I want you to try and see what I see in it, just once."

My dad's stern face broke into a wide smile and he nodded his head and then embraced me. "I do love yer, son," he said in a low voice and just like that he'd agreed to come with us to the game. And what a game! United versus the Wednesday.

The atmosphere in the room had completely changed. Everyone felt more relaxed and we were now all standing together.

"Will you be coming with us, Rab?" my dad said.

"Nah, I'm not sure the Wednesday or United would want me there. Besides, I've finished my business with Jack, so I need to get the train back to Preston before my people up there wonder where I am."

"I'm very pleased I had the chance to meet with you, Mr Howell," I said.

"Same here, little *mush*. If you're ever in Preston or I'm back down here, come and see me. Oh, I almost forgot…" He handed me a cardboard box. "These are for you."

I opened the lid. Inside were a pair of football boots. They looked brand new.

"Jack here said you were the same size as me. He reckoned you'd find a use for them."

I was speechless. All I could do was nod and shake his hand. Eventually I managed to get a 'thank you' to come out of my mouth.

On the way back home that evening, with an old carriage lamp Uncle Jack had lent us to light our way, I felt like I was floating. I had met my hero, he'd given me a pair of his boots and, according to Uncle Jack, we'd seen one of the best matches ever – even though

United lost. Having my dad cheering and shouting and enjoying football beside me was incredible. After the referee had blown the whistle and we were walking out of the stadium I said, "What did you think, Dad?"

"Well, it was no horse race, but that wasn't half as bad as I thought it would be," my dad replied.

"Never seen you leap in the air shouting your head off at a horse race, Dad," I replied with a grin.

"All right, all right, it was *kushti*," my dad said, ruffling my hair.

I could never have imagined things turning out like this. It was like a fairy tale. A football fairy tale.

Eighteen

It was good for everyone to be back together again. My dad and Uncle Jack were doing business once more and looking forward to getting the foal they were going to train up to be their racing horse. They had already chosen his name: Chiriclo. "He will fly like a bird," my dad declared.

I was working for Uncle Jack delivering things to and from his shops and the other businesses he'd bought.

We talked about football most of the time and, as a result, even my dad had started following the Sheffield United games. I was pleased to be able to reconnect with my football-playing friends from school, even though I wasn't going any more. They couldn't believe it when I told them about meeting Rab Howell and demanded I bring the boots to show them. Joe and Samuel's faces were a picture.

A few weeks in, as I was getting my list of deliveries and pick-ups from Uncle Jack he said, "I saw Harry yesterday. He was asking about you – how

155

fit you were and whether you'd still be interested in having a game."

I believed that Harry understood about the wedding and was prepared to give me a second chance, but I wasn't sure about the lads in the team. I'd had enough hostility before I'd let them down. Maybe I'd be better off with a fresh start with a new team.

Uncle Jack was good at reading my mood, "I know you're worried about how some of the lads might be about you coming back – truth is some of them still haven't forgiven you – but Harry has warned them to give you a second chance or else."

I didn't ask what the 'or else' was.

"Thing is, Lijah, it's no ordinary game. It's an important game. There's a lot riding on it and it's in less than three weeks. At least two of the lads are being watched by professional clubs. This is, in a way, a trial for a contract; one of them is being watched for the future and Harry ... not sure I should be telling you this ... if he can win the game he's been near enough promised a manager's job at a proper club. He can give up his job in the mill."

I thought about Rab Howell, what he'd achieved and how he'd told me you have to take risks sometimes, otherwise you'll never know what you could accomplish, especially in sport.

"Tell him I'll do it and ask him when I can start training," I replied.

"No time like the present, Lijah. Let's go and see him now ... oh and by the way, Lijah, the lad being watched for the future is you!"

As we travelled down to see Harry, I was both excited and nervous. As we got closer to the playing field, there was also a sense of dread creeping into my thoughts. We called at Harry's house and then all three of us walked to the football pitch. He and Uncle Jack talked about the upcoming game. I didn't try and join in the conversation; I just carried the football Harry had given me as we left his house.

Uncle Jack had already told me that Harry wanted to test my fitness and skill level before the other players turned up.

The piece of fairly ordinary grass that doubled as a football pitch in the season held bad memories for me, but I knew I had to try and overcome them.

Harry took the ball off me and walked to one end of the pitch, which was marked as a goal. He threw the ball towards me.

"All right – try and get one past me," he said. Even though Harry was older than my dad, he was still fit and – according to Uncle Jack – he had been a good goalkeeper in his day. I started to dribble the ball towards him. About twenty yards out he shouted, "Shoot from there!" I did as he said. He moved quickly and caught it in his hands.

"Not bad, plenty of power," he said as he drop-kicked the ball back to me. I caught it on my chest, ran forward and hit it hard. Harry had no chance of stopping this one. It went past him like a speeding train.

"I'll give yer that one," he said, smiling. "Now run up and down. I want to see how fit you are."

I ran and ran, backwards and forwards, up and down the pitch. I even started to put some swerves into my run, as if I was dodging around opponents.

"All right lad, I've seen enough. You're in."

"Thank you," I said, as relief swept through me.

"Told you, Harry, this lad is a talent. Almost a season away from the game and he's come back even better. I'm telling you, he's the next Rab Howell."

Harry nodded. "Don't let that talent go to yer head. Some of the lads ain't forgotten how yer played last time."

Some of the lads who turned up to practice were pleased to see me, but some of them weren't and they showed it by trying to get rough in the training session. Luckily, Harry spotted it and put a stop to it.

At the end of the session, Harry got us all together.

"Lijah is back training with us," he said. "I want him to play in the Cup game. If anyone has a problem with that, they'd better tell me now." He looked around at everyone, waiting to see if anyone spoke up, but no one did.

"Right, that's settled then. And another thing – I want you all to keep quiet about how good this lad is; he's going to be our secret weapon," he said as he tapped his nose. I was a good player but because I hadn't played for any teams hardly anyone knew me. I could see what Harry was doing, hoping he had the element of surprise. I knew enough about football now to know winning was as much about unsettling the other players' mental game plan as it was their physical game.

My training with the team had gone well. I was as ready as I could be for the game. Everyone from my family who was really important to me was going to be watching. My dad had not only agreed to come, but had started to try and give me advice, even though he hardly knew anything about the sport.

On the day of the match, my dad, Henry, Genty, Uncle Billy, Auntie Britti, my mam and even my *phuri dai* were all standing watching as me and the rest of the team came out of our huddle with Harry's instructions still ringing in our ears. I spied Samuel and Joe who both gave me a beaming smile and clapped their hands. I nodded and smiled back.

The game started off slowly, each team playing defensively, knowing what was riding on the outcome. I don't know whether I was intimidated by the size of some of the players on the opposing team, or whether I felt that there were some in my own team who weren't supporting me when I had the ball, or whether it was the fact that my family were watching, me, but whatever the reason, I wasn't playing as well as I could.

I had a decent shot on goal and sliced it, which means it went wide. I could feel the confidence I had when I started slowly draining away. I glanced at my dad, who just looked confused, maybe wondering why I hadn't scored a goal yet.

Then the game became rougher. One of the big forwards shoulder-charged me as another player aimed a kick at my shin. I went down as he carried on and scored their first goal. As they were celebrating, I saw Uncle Jack having to restrain my dad, who was clearly all for coming on to the pitch and sorting the big lad out.

The game didn't improve much before half-time was called, but at least the other team didn't score again.

Harry was not best pleased with any of us. "What the hell do yer think yer playing at? You look like you don't even want to win." He looked straight at me. "Do you want to be a footballer or not? If you don't pick it up in the second half, I'm going to take yer off."

I didn't want to go home a loser in front of my family. I was almost paralysed with fear. Harry looked at his watch. "We've less than five minutes. Get a drink and get ready. Do not let me – or yourselves – down."

Uncle Jack came over to me and, reaching into the inside pocket of his overcoat, he handed me an envelope. "I forgot to give you this."

I looked at the envelope with my name on it. It had Uncle Jack's address and a Preston postmark.

"Open it then," Uncle Jack said.

I ripped it open and took out a letter. Immediately, I started to read.

Dear Lijah,

It was a great pleasure to meet you at Jack Davis's house. I can't write very well so have got someone else to put down my words. Jack tells me you are a decent reader, so I hope this finds you well.

The sport you have chosen – that has chosen you – is not for the faint-hearted, especially for

Romani people. You are going to have to fight
every step of the way. In every tough spot, you
must think of your family and all the Romani
people from the past who had a much harder life, so
you can have the opportunities you have got now.

Jack is a good man, and he will guide you well,
but in any game you play you have to show your
Traveller heart.

Good luck and God bless,
Rab Howell

I folded the letter and put it back into the envelope, handing it over to Uncle Jack just as Harry called us back to get ready for the second half.

The words in the letter had gone straight to my brain and heart like a lightning charge. As soon as I was back on the field, my body and my vision were locked on the ball.

I was in the woods again. That ball was mine and no one was going to stop me. I ran like a racehorse and jumped like a deer. No one could catch me!

I had the ball at my feet, close enough to shoot. The goal was the hole in the tree and I struck the ball with all the force I could muster. The guardian in the goal didn't even see it go past him. I looked over to my family. They were jumping up and down and shouting my name. Harry and Uncle Jack were doing the same. The other team's trainer looked like he was in shock.

No sooner had the game kicked off again, I had the ball back to my feet. I could feel my team get behind me, doing the sequences we'd practised in training. I passed the ball, got it back, passed it again and, as it sailed over to me, I hit it in mid-air, twisting my body and leaping like a salmon. As I fell to the ground, I saw the ball fly into the goal.

My teammates were shaking my hand now and patting me on the back. But I hadn't finished yet. Two goals was a good start, but I wanted a hat-trick.

I could tell the keeper thought I was going to let another speeding shot fly, but I didn't. Instead, I went closer and closer, forcing him to come out to meet me and, when he did, I sent him the wrong way and just tapped the ball into the goal. My family went wild, shouting louder than ever.

"You're a blummin' hero!" Harry shouted, but I knew who the real hero was.

Nineteen

Once all the fuss had died down over the football match, we got on with our usual lives, which, in reality, were very unusual. I carried on working with my dad, but something had changed for the better. He'd never be a true football supporter, but he was a supporter of me playing the game and that was all I'd ever wanted.

When we told stories around the fire, my dad would sometimes tell the tale of the football match where his son scored three goals and use the term hat-trick and tell people why it was called that. Every time my dad told it, I became more of a hero. To listen to him, you'd have thought I was playing in a world-class stadium against a team of killer giants on my own, rather than an ordinary team game on some fairly rough grass between houses and factories. It made me feel good that he was proud of my achievements and that he was now as ambitious as I was for me to fulfil my potential in the sport.

My Uncle Billy would get in on the act too,

joking about me becoming a famous football player and building a caravan that looked like a mansion, or living in a castle with a butler and everyone having to call me "sir" like a gentleman or a lord.

"The lord of football," he said one night and everyone laughed until my mam told us all off.

"There's only one Lord and he's got nothing to do with football, Billy," she said. He immediately went quiet and then said "sorry, Kushy", but then Mam winked, so we knew she'd only been joking. We laughed even harder after that.

I loved nights like that: where we just sat around the fire and enjoyed who we were. Knowing that we had each other meant we had the world.

Uncle Jack was very much part of our lives. He'd helped Genty and Henry get their shop and they were now living above it with their new baby, who they'd named Little Henry after his dad. My mam was always round there, helping them out with the baby, so Henry and Genty could get on with building their business. We all helped out where we could.

Our family was moving on with Henry and Genty's shop, but also my football playing. My dad and Uncle Jack were talking about setting up a business that hired out horses and carts. It felt like we were definitely part of the twentieth century.

My dad was keen that we didn't forget where we had come from. There were no history books that told the real story of Romanies, so he felt it was important that he kept reminding us of it. It was no hardship listening to my dad. Some people made up stories about us – some of them were plain daft, but it didn't stop other *Gorjas* believing them. But as long as we knew the truth, that would do for now.

One night, just as my dad was about to tell us a tale, Genty, holding little Henry on her knee, said thoughtfully, "Maybe, one day in the future when he's all growed up our Little Henry here might become a scholar and write proper books about us."

I wasn't sure about that as clever as Henry and Genty were. I couldn't imagine their son or any Romani writing books, but before Rab Howell became the first Romani footballer to play for England, that probably seemed like an impossibility too.

As much as I loved all the history in our past, I desperately wanted to get on with the future. I kept playing football with my friends and some competitive games with Harry's team, but it was clear that, as good as they were, they were never going to be any more than a good local team for that part of Sheffield. Harry unfortunately didn't get the pro manager job he wanted and that had impacted on the team too. I wanted and needed more.

I kept training, kept learning and looked forward to my letters from my hero and mentor Rab Howell. I held on to the belief that I would get an opportunity sooner or later and that I would be ready for it when it came.

We'd hear rumours that there was a scout keeping his eye on me. After every match, I'd get all excited, wondering if someone might come up and talk to me, and then nothing would happen. Uncle Jack and my dad kept telling me to be patient. I was young and there was plenty of time, and Sheffield was the best place to be in terms of football. To hear them talk about it, it was as if this city was the centre of the football world. I wasn't so sure and wondered if I should try another town – pretend I wasn't a Romani, maybe even get a job like Henry had done.

It was just very frustrating, knowing you had a talent and were a very good player, but not being able to get on the next rung of the ladder.

There were days when I seriously thought of giving up, but then there was always something to keep me going, to keep me believing that I could do it. I could be a footballer.

Twenty

Uncle Jack came up to our latest camp just after my mam and dad had left to go and help Henry and Genty out with their shop. It always seemed to be busy whenever I visited and Genty said they were doing a very good trade.

I was repairing one of the old carts that had been bought for the horse and cart hire business. I had built up a bit of a reputation as decent footballer around Sheffield and Uncle Jack had helped me every step of the way, but my age was against me. A lot of clubs said I was too young or too small or both. I was getting impatient and felt if I didn't get signed by a club soon, I'd lose my motivation for the whole thing and have to find something else to do with my future.

"I've got some good news for you, Lijah," said Uncle Jack. "I've got you a trial at a new outfit – Ecclesedge. There's money behind them and they've got big plans. I think you're ready, do you?"

"I am, Uncle," I said with confidence. "When's the trial?"

"Next Friday evening," he said.

"Marvellous," I said.

The time leading up to my try-out with Ecclesedge went both slow and fast. During the day, I had all my chores to do and then at night, lying in my tent, I just couldn't get to sleep, thinking about what it could mean. What if I wasn't good enough? Whatever happened, it was going to change my life for ever, I was sure of that.

I'd asked around about this new outfit, Ecclesedge. They already had some good players and, like Uncle Jack had said, big plans. League plans, trophies and taking on the big boys.

I'd agreed to meet Uncle Jack at the trial, mainly because I wanted time to gather my thoughts and walking over there would give me that time. Lots of things were going through my mind. Doubts were creeping in, but I just kept trying to tell myself: "Just give it a go and at least you'll know one way or the other. What have you got to lose?"

What I had to lose would be the ability to play football properly – to do it as a job. What if I wasn't as good as other people thought I was? As *I* thought I was? I knew that would be a huge blow, but I continued to talk myself around, focusing on all the good games I'd had.

Once at the club and seeing that I'd be on a proper pitch, I was in a better frame of mind. I started to get fixed on the task in hand, whatever it turned out to be. I soon realized that I wasn't the only one having a trial. I counted eight other lads and there was a handful of the proper players on the pitch. Their coach, a man who was their trainer, spoke to each of us, confirming our names and what position we liked to play, and then got us all together and made us run up and down the pitch while he timed us on his silver pocket watch. A couple of the others were soon out of breath, bent over and trying to get some much-needed air into their lungs. I kept on running, until the coach blew his whistle for us to stop. Then we went on to the field and took shots at the goal. Finally, we had a little game against each other.

It might have seemed like a little game to others, but I put everything into it that I could. Rab Howell had told me that every game, no matter where and when you played it, was a big game.

At the end of the session, the coach went to have a word with the regular players and another man who looked like he had some role in running the club.

He then spoke quietly to each of the eight other

lads before finally coming over to me, where I'd been joined by Uncle Jack.

"All right, Jack," the coach said.

"Never better, Cyril, What did you think about our lad here?"

Cyril looked me up and down. "He's not bad. Better than any of them who've come along today. He's a bit small though."

I was fed up with hearing this and felt my fists bunching.

"Size isn't everything, Cyril. You've seen he's strong as a bull," Uncle Jack said.

"Aye, I've heard them Gypsies bring 'em up tough."

I couldn't stop myself reacting to that. "I'm a Romani person, sir. I'd prefer to be known as that"

"Hey, lad, I didn't mean nowt by it. I like yer spirit and yer have some good skills, but I've no use for anyone with a temper," Cyril said.

My first reaction was to wonder whether I even wanted to play for a man like this, but Rab Howell had warned me I was going to come up against attitudes like this wherever I went: "Just like on the pitch, you have to pick your battles. You can't tackle everyone. The only way we're going to change people's minds and hearts is by showing them who we really are, it's not fair but it's how it is." Rab's wise advice came to me and I kept my mouth shut.

"I've been saying for a while, with the right training, he will be a very good player. And he's got ambition," Uncle Jack said.

"What's yer ambition, lad?" Cyril asked.

I thought I had nothing to lose if he laughed at me, so I just said what I felt. "I'm going to be the next Rab Howell, sir: be in the papers, win a cup, play for me country even and make me a good livin' from it."

"I like yer confidence, lad, and I'm prepared to take you on over the winter as a reserve – see how yer do. Yer have to come to all the trainings and be ready for any match. You'll have to spend the whole match just watching if that's what I decide. Oh, and there's some money in it for yer, but you'll have to carry on working."

Uncle Jack looked at me and raised his eyebrows as if to say, "Over to you, Lijah."

"I'll take it, sir," I said, putting out my hand to shake his.

"Call me gaffer from now on, lad, I'm your boss."

I'd never had a boss in my life before; it was going to take a bit of getting used to.

I felt sorry for the other lads who tried out for the team and didn't get in, but I was just so happy for myself and Uncle Jack. It'd been a long journey to get here and he'd been with me every step of the way.

On my first match day, I was told to stand at the edge of the pitch until called. I was so excited to be there looking at the pitch so green and so flat, both teams in proper football kits, with their supporters at opposite ends cheering them on. The atmosphere was fabulous. There were a couple of other reserve players who watched the game for the first ten minutes, then started to laugh and joke with each other. I kept my focus on the game, watching my team kick, tackle and try to score. I watched what worked and what didn't. I even studied the spectators for their reactions.

Uncle Jack came to stand with me, but not a word was exchanged between us until the half-time interval, when he told me he'd noticed how intently I'd been watching the game. "Didn't want to break yer concentration," he said.

"I reckon it's the only way to learn more. And I want to find out who the best player is and get better than him," I said.

Uncle Jack laughed. "You've been listening well to what I said, lad, haven't yer?"

He was right. He'd taught me so much about football since I'd first met him, always reading me sports stories from the newspapers, explaining the latest rules, telling me how to do moves better and to think ahead in the game. Rab Howell had taught me to be thankful for any help people gave me, but to always remember that it was my hard work and dedication that got me where I was, and no one could ever take the credit for that.

As cold as it was just standing there, I watched the second half just as intently. I knew that I wasn't going to get a game; no one had asked me to get changed or even put my boots on. I also knew that the gaffer was testing me to see how much patience I had. Uncle Jack had warned me that might happen.

"Been a bit of a wasted day for yer, new boy," one of the other reserves said mockingly.

"I've heard he's more used to playing with bears in the woods," said the other, sniggering.

"Nah, I've enjoyed it," I said, and I meant it. I pushed my anger down and tried to ignore what they were both trying to do. They had no idea how many years I'd dealt with this kind of rubbish and how many fights I'd had over it. My first reaction was to teach them both a lesson with my fists, but Uncle Jack had warned me about keeping my temper in check and being professional.

I didn't rise to their bait; I just ignored them, rose above it. Rab Howell had warned me that being a

Romani footballer was going to be tough and I was going to have to put up with name calling.

"You make sure you're here on Tuesday after work for training," Cyril said.

"Yes, sir," I said.

"Gaffer," he corrected me.

As I changed back into my everyday clothes in the changing room, I felt every inch a proper footballer. My mind wandered back to that day in school when I first kicked a ball and then to meeting my hero Rab Howell, and now to playing for an ambitious club. I may not have played in this match, but there would be others and I knew I *would* get to play. First Ecclesedge, then who knew where? I was determined to make everyone proud – especially myself.

DICTIONARY OF ROMANI TERMS

baro – big

bitti – little

chavo – boy

chavvies – children

dinlo – fool

gav – town

Gorja – non-Gypsy person

Gypsy – a legal term in England to describe Romani people or 'persons of nomadic habit of life whatever their race or origin'. However, when used with negative words before it, the word can become offensive. The shortened term of 'gyppo' is highly offensive and should never be used

habben – food

hawked – knocking on doors to sell or buy things

ladged – embarrassed

jall – go

jall ter woodrus – go to bed

juk – dog

kushti – good

kushti folki – good people

lovver – money

meskie – tea

moskerers – police

mullered – killed

mush – man

nak – nose

phrala – brother

phuri dai – grandmother

quoits – a game of skill where horseshoes are thrown, aiming to land over a metal stake

radge/radgeness – stupid/stupidity

rokker – talk

Rumness – the Romani language (also 'Romanes')

shoddy – old material that was recycled and used as stuffing in furniture and to make new utility clothes and army uniforms

tattin – collecting old clothes and cloth

vardos – horse-drawn caravans (from the Persian 'vordon' for cart)

wafti – bad

woodrus – bed

wonga – money

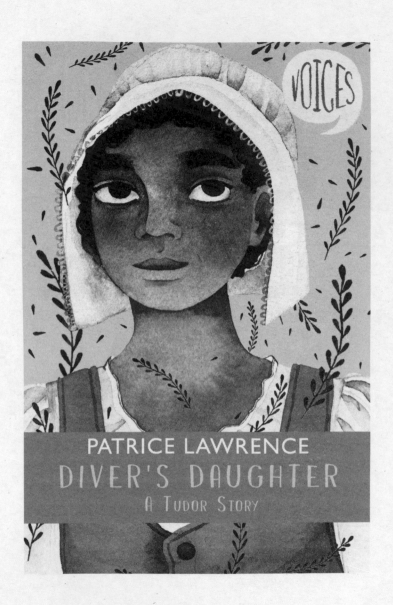

PATRICE LAWRENCE

DIVER'S DAUGHTER

A Tudor Story

EMPIRE'S END
A ROMAN STORY
LEILA RASHEED

SON OF THE CIRCUS

A VICTORIAN STORY

E.L. NORRY

TWO SISTERS
A STORY OF FREEDOM
KEREEN GETTEN

BENJAMIN ZEPHANIAH

EMPIRE WINDRUSH

'An invaluable story for young readers who want to learn about the Windrush generation's experience.'

Alex Wheatle

WINDRUSH CHILD